Ruthie Has a New Love

Anne Wilensky

To order this book
Go to www.createspace.com/3394409
Author's bio, plus book description, and cover pic are also there

Or order at Amazon.com

Or ask your local bookstore

Published by Haiku Helen Press
Cover design by Helen Kritzler aka Haiku Helen
Drawings on front cover and back cover by Helen Kritzer

ISBN
978-0-9840976-0-9
0-98409776-0-0

Printed in the United States of America.

Thank you

I want to thank everyone in New York and everyone in Tucson

Ya'll have been very good to me

I have been helped in infinite ways by all of you, and this includes everyone I have been on internet forums with

I am very fortunate

I love you

Anne

for all

Let our Arizona sunshine come to you wherever you are with its exceptional brilliance and warmth. And make every day a joy for you. Love, Annie

Chapters

Chapters from forthcoming novels

November 3

Ruthie has a new love

It's a pretty blue sky. A soft blue, not a hard deep blue. The soft blue of fairy tale illustration, or how a mom might paint the ceiling for nursery for her new baby, the soft blue which goes with his yellow fluffy duckies. I can even see way to the north, soft white clouds just above the mountains. And the light seems very yellow. Maybe November has a lot of yellow light to it. I don't see or feel any breezes, the leaves stirred for an instant, it was as if they murmured. There must have been a teeny breeze. But now all is still. It's actually quite a peaceful morning. Sparrows are flitting in and out of the trees out my window but they are not making a sound. Hahaha there is a tableau feeling.

It actually seems like rare weather because there is an intermission feeling about it. It is not fresh vivid refreshing passionate alive. It is as soft as pretty soft blue sky, as soft as the nursery awaiting the new baby. And nothing could be quieter. It's like a rest note in music. If time just stopped it would be like this. Movement would cease. It's as if the world stopped and we all stepped right out of the world. But not completely. Sparrows alight occasionally and take off occasionally. The birds stir in the world which is not stirring.

Well my friend Ruthie is having a love affair. For 18 years her life has been raising her son. She has not thought about love affairs, looked for love affairs, wanted one or expected one. And now she is having one and she is thrilled.

When I first met Ruthie she was in her mid-twenties, I was in my early twenties and our whole life was love affairs. It was the milieu we lived in, the ocean we swam in. Life was all love affairs. Either having one, wanting one, waiting for one, looking for one. All the cycles of love affairs. That was where our mind was. No matter what else we were doing or thinking, love affairs was the mainspring of our life then. We were all about love affairs.

All these years later, it's like we are rose buds which flowered into magnificent roses. Who could have dreamed then, when we were teachers together at PS 110 on the

Lower East Side, that we would be where we are now and who we are now. Life bloomed and bloomed and bloomed for us. Ruthie is in San Diego with her 18 year old son, and if she had any dreams at all, I think it was that her son Davy would not leave home. She likes Davy, she likes living with him, she likes the companionship and family.

And of course I am still with Bill and the delicate balancing act which a relationship is. My learning school has been marriage. Ruthie was naive idealistic and jealous of her friends who had long-term relationships until she got married at 44. When she fled to San Diego with little Davy 10 years later to get away from her marriage, her attitude changed. She hasn't looked for a love affair since and hasn't been sure if she wanted one.

There was a lot of happiness and fulfillment in her marriage too, and she remains best friends and deeply close with her former husband. But when marriage turns traumatic, it is traumatic. Ruthie's friends, me included, chose to weather out the trauma. We are still with the guy. But Ruthie fled to San Diego. It seems to me Ruthie is blooming in all kinds of new ways in San Diego. It's as if Ruthie is a gardenia. I never realized she was a tropical flower when she lived with Roberto and Baby Davy in Flushing.

Because Bill and I moved to Tucson 6 months after Davy's first birthday, I really missed the whole era of Ruthie, Roberto, and Davy in Flushing. The last time I saw Ruthie and Davy, Davy was still in his stroller, and Ruthie and I sat in MacDonald's with him, and she told me about Davy's birthday party, he ate a balloon. 6 months later I fled to Tucson, but I took my husband and dog with me. And 8 years later, Ruthie fled to San Diego with Davy, to get away from her husband. You could say things did not work out. But of course Ruthie's other friends, me and Joan and Pat, were up against the same problems and we worked them out. And so there is always choice.

Roberto had been married before Ruthie, and had two daughters with his first wife. She couldn't take the problem and she left Roberto. So he met Ruthie who he adored. He was 13 years younger than Ruthie and passionate about her. They met and married within the same week. And it was a beautiful marriage, until it didn't work out, then Ruthie fled.

And finally Roberto accepted it, and married again, and has a new baby. He is completely loving lovely nice man, wonderful husband, and very hard working. He just has some problems, as who of us do not. His first wife didn't want to put up with them, Ruthie decided not to either, but his 3rd wife is hanging in there. Ruthie is close to her on the phone too. Because Roberto stayed in the Flushing co-op Ruthie's mom bought for both of them when they first married.

So Roberto who was born in Venezuela and spent his whole life there, till Ruthie came down to visit and he married her, has been living all this time in Apartment 3G in Dara Gardens. Ruthie is in San Diego. And I am in Tucson. Roberto wound up the only one who is a New Yorker. And I remember when Ruthie was first teaching him English and he was learning his way around New York. He had never been to America before.

But Roberto is the New Yorker now. Ruthie is the San Diegan and I am the desert rat. It is as if we all switched places. Roberto is in the cold northern mega city. Ruthie is on a tropical coast, and I am on the subtropical desert. Roberto who had never owned a winter coat in his life, is now the only one with a winter coat. And Ruthie and I who grew up in winter coats, have forgotten what they are like.

All the news we now get of our former hometown comes from Roberto. He is taxi cab driver and calls Ruthie from his cell phone. And Ruthie tells me.

Ruthie remains close with all of Roberto's family. He brought them all to New York. His brother is now a very successful dentist here making lots of money. And Roberto's sister, Ruthie adores. I see now how much love there is between Roberto and Ruthie, and Ruthie and Roberto's whole family.

Davy may be in San Diego, but Ruthie is very close to his father and his father's family. Ruthie's talent for making connections and keeping connections, that web of closeness she brings, has miraculously kept this whole family together in their own way. She is close to Roberto's new wife too. But her favorite of favorites is Roberto's sister.

Davy really does have a lot of family back in New York. And when Ruthie first took him to San Diego when he was 9, he did miss New York. But now he is 100 per cent Southern Californian and loves it there. It took a while. But it took a while for all of us. Ruthie and Davy, me and Bill, we all left New York and it was a big change.

I don't know how to describe Ruthie's attitude about her new love affair, except there is a hush and holiness about it.

As if deep in a snow and ice filled forest, she happened across a beautiful blue violet with green leaves. A miracle in the snowy forest. With a happy butterfly lit on it. All of sweet happy warm spring suddenly happened upon in a snow and ice forest. If it had been a tiny fairy she found, she could not have been more surprised and delighted, than finding warm happy flowery spring. Exactly when she didn't expect to.

She sent me on email a photo of her and her new boyfriend, and she is wearing pearls and looking very pretty. I never saw Ruthie in a pearl necklace before. But she hasn't been a girlfriend in a long time. Ruthie looks like a girlfriend, pretty in her pearl necklace.

November 4

The Prince Arrives

Today's blue sky is a deeper blue, pristine and cloudless like yesterday. Altho again I see the puffy white clouds off in distance above the mountains. They rise slowly and eventually will dot our blue sky. The air is a drop cooler now, there is a fresh cool air current. The blue is a prettier blue, deeper and more crystalline, its clarity and deeper hue bring the beauty into the day. And the fresh cool air current gives it its life. Today is perkier day than yesterday. The train whistles off in the distance.

The cool air current comes in my open window and blows on my bare shoulders, even kisses my face, and makes the leaves move ever so slightly.

Ruthie's new love, Tom Starr, is as far from her type, as it would be far from my type to fall in love with a Tibetan. My love life did not last long compared to Ruthie's, I met Bill at 25 and love life adventures ended, then marriage began. But I would describe my type, looking back on it, as they always looked like they came from Cleveland. Just a few inches taller than me with light brown hair. And shy, I liked shy boys. Ruthie's type was the reverse, she liked short chubby boys, either from foreign countries or from Harlem. Al's mother had danced at the Cotton Club. Roberto was from Venezuela, she had boyfriends from the Near East, and all those Mexican boyfriends when she lived in Mexico.

If she is living in San Diego now, one would think her new boyfriend would be short chubby Portuguese. But Tom Starr is exceedingly tall, and thin, and is a Cockney from London. Ruthie could not be more surprised.

She met him at coffee shop one morning few weeks ago. And something must have really happened then, because a few days later she called to tell me about the love affair.

She said "after we had coffee together, and the attraction was so intense, I didn't ask anyone about him; in Ocean Beach everyone knows everyone, and I would have heard so much."

But it turns out Tom did ask about Ruthie, and Ruthie reported "everyone told him she is a toughie." Which shows how appearances are deceiving, as no one could be more of a softie and sweetie than Ruthie, as I am sure Tom found out for himself.

It began off with intense physical attraction and it is a hot sex affair, altho Ruthie doesn't talk about that part of it. What has melted her heart is his protectiveness towards her, and his sensitivity. There is no question Ruthie's heart has melted. This is an affair of the heart.

Ruthie who has never fallen in love before, is in love.

It has transformed her whole life. Now she is a planet going around a central sun.

One day she saw his angry side so she broke up with him. "I already was married to an angry man, I don't want another angry man" she said.

He said "I wanted to show you all my sides so you would really know me, I want to be completely open with you."

Ruthie said "if you are free to be angry then it means I have total freedom too."

And he said "good!"

So Tom became angry, Ruthie became upset, and it was resolved by both of them claiming absolute freedom for themselves, and giving absolute freedom to each other. What could be better, there is love and freedom.

I guess they are still in the wonderful period of discovery about each other. She loved it when she discovered his smile lit up his whole face. She loved it when she showed him on her computer, he can talk on phone to his sister in England for two cents a minute. And he got on and giggled and giggled with his sister, he loves her so much.

Ruthie and I did ask her Higher Self about him on the phone. And her Higher Self said, "Ruthie will have to decide if she will trust Tom with her whole heart, her whole sensitivity, her whole life. She keeps her sensitivity hidden, she hasn't trusted anyone with it. And Tom won't be happy in the relationship unless it is a full one, and she allows him to know and be close to her sensitivity."

Ruthie said "I have not been in love since fourth grade when I was in love with David Adelman, everything since then has been a crush. And with Roberto one day we met and next day we were married, we never had being in love."

And there in Ruthie's 4th grade class picture is little Ruthie, as sweet and open and shy as a flower, a happy yellow buttercup. And then the next picture is Ruthie as a teenager, and you can see the shell put over her sensitivity.

So I guess that is the real story of what is going on now. Her soul must be crying out to have its sensitivity released, free, open to view, and expressed. And the only way that can happen is from Tom. Only a love affair can do that. The Prince who awakens Sleeping Beauty. Tom may not look or sound like Prince Charming-- Ruthie's age, Cockney accent, tall as a bean pole.. And that English face which rarely smiles, but when it does lights up the universe. This is a soul adventure. And Tom is sent to free Ruthie from the prison she has put her sensitivity in. As her Higher Self said "it may take great courage for Ruthie to finally do it, to trust Tom with all her sensitivity."

But this is a bona fide adventure. Ruthie is adventuring into the unknown. A major transformation this way comes....

P.S. And there could not be any doubt who David Adelman was. 9 year old Ruthie had festooned his picture with hearts, in their 4th grade class picture.

P.P.S. "What will Tom think when he comes to my house" she said after their 3rd meeting. "He lives in a cabin, I live in a big fancy house…"

November 5

Change

Well an election has come and gone and today the cold weather arrived in Tucson. I am sitting in front of my open window in two skirts and a long sleeve jersey top, watching my dog look for things to nibble on in backyard. The sky is the palest of blues, as there seems to be a damp chilly cloud cover in front of it.

O now Beanie has his dog biscuit in his mouth. He found it in the spot he buried it yesterday and is carrying it around to find a better spot. There is relief in the change of weather, altho cold and damp is not nearly as lovely as warm and dry. But winter always arrives early on the desert and leaves early too. This is the time when winter starts arriving. And there is always relief when what is going to happen does happen. To be facing it instead of dreading it. And it is not that bad really now that it is here, and there is refreshment in the change.

When the change does come you realize that deep at the bottom of everything you wanted change. Simply because change, whatever it is, is fresh new start. There comes a point when everyone wants a fresh new chapter to open up in their life, for the past to be forgotten and the new to start, and today is the start of the new.

Yes nothing seems to be going my way. In 10 days all the public pools in Tucson will close till April (I like to swim every day.) The city made a surprise decision to save money on heating the pools by closing them, but one will be open. Which is fine unless it is overcrowded for swimming. We will wait and see and hope for the best.

It is possible that all the changes-- even tho I am overjoyed change happened and the new world starts right this instant-- the only changes obvious now are not what anyone wanted. Swim pools closing, warmth and light decreasing, and the election on the local level did not go my way. But I can't get away from the feeling that today marks the start of the new. And what was, isn't anymore, so all new must be there.

And who knows, if a new ocean wave is rolling in, what kinds of treasures it will hold? There may be good surprises in there, things I haven't thought of that I might like, as well as things I've wanted for long time. The fact is there is tremendous potential with the new, because it means whatever arrives will be different from what was. And to be honest the old had to be gotten out of the way for the new to arrive, to make the space for it.

Today is the day of transition. I woke up counting my losses, but I was surprisingly at peace about it, because even as I was counting my losses, I was wrapping my mind around them. I knew it meant out with the old, in with the new. And how could I not speculate about the new advantages, even before it occurred to me to get my hopes up that something wonderful could arrive in the new, when the new just seemed like hard luck and bad. It is still the new. It still means whole other ballgame. And there must be something in how our spirit is made to welcome whole other ballgame. Our spirit must be made in freshness to appreciate freshness when it arrives, even when it arrives under the colors of "well my team lost."

I didn't get in who I wanted, but the other team is cheering, they got in their guys. But win or lose it's on with the new, that season is over, new one has begun.

Naturally in the final play-offs it grabs all your attention. But once it is decided our attention moves off. Today is transition day so my attention is still on absorbing the loss. I went from cheering wildly for my team to win to absorbing the loss today. But I still think, once the loss is absorbed, my attention will move off to other things. And it is starting to occur to me to realize where attention is, there is my life. I will have a new life because my attention will be on completely different things, and that is good.

I never realized before, win or lose, it is decided-- the advantage that it be decided and that I can move on. I've always been so attached to outcome before. But maybe that is natural and right too in its own way. Why not put all your energy into the outcome you want, until it is decided, and then of course you are free to move on.

And that things may not always be what they appear either. I put every ounce of my effort at the beginning of the summer that our basset hound Lulu would stay with us and not go to Heaven. But outcome went the other way. It seemed like tragic loss to me. But I read in *Letter from God* yesterday or the day before, God said "what the world calls bad is good. Leaving your body is a good thing, not a bad thing."

So how can I be so sure this new team which took over is a bad thing to happen, it could be a good thing to happen.

Clearly God sees with different eyes than the world when he says leaving your body is a good thing not a bad thing. But I trust God sees with the eyes of reality.

So who knows maybe God sees winter arriving as good thing not bad thing. New government as good thing not bad thing. Shutting all the city pools save one as good thing not bad thing. If I am willing to concede God might be right on the biggest thing of all, Lulu, then why not have new attitude 'bout all these most minor of things.

If the overcrowding at the one open city pool is too intense, I can always join the JCC for the winter. And I might even win the Lottery to pay for the JCC. It just feels like a good time to be playing the lottery religiously, when it is the time of the new and you don't know what new will come into your life. Most expansion costs dough, and dough is what the Lottery brings, if luck goes your way....

Love, Anne

P.S. My own friend in Tucson had run for office. I thought she would be great. I was upset when she lost. But I now see things work out for the best in their own way.

November 6

Novel in a Month

Winter is here. It happened over night. I am sitting here freezing before my open window, even tho I am wearing lots of layers. And last night I slept under two quilts plus added an extra blanket.

Of course it is thrilling. Winter is thrilling. It will warm up later in the day when the sun comes out and rises high in the sky. Our desert sun is big bright warm. It is a major source of heat in winter. As long as one is in the sunshine and it has risen high enough in the sky, one is always toasty warm. But it starts to descend earlier in winter. By 3 pm it is no longer that wonderful supply of heat. But the 4 hours it warms and delights is enough to take the edge off the whole thing. To know that if one waits long enough in the very early morning, eventually we can walk out into another season.

Winter is not a 24 hour business on the desert. As long as the sun is out, which is most days, we do get several hours of a Maine summer. One can shed all those layers, walk out into sunshine, and sunbathe happily in a sundress.

We only look forward to end of winter so much, and winter does end very early on desert, because when we are not sunbathing we are always chilly. And while it is true the cold is invigorating, this is a southern hot land, we are not used to being chilly, we are used to being relaxed and comfortable when we are not too warm. Being chilly is really off our radar, and it is always a surprise when winter comes.

When we walked into Jerry's pool late yesterday, late for our swim, it was only open for another half hour, a man was at the desk talking to Jerry with two of the sweetest dogs in the world, each on a long leash. I thought they were his dogs. And they both wagged their tails when they saw me and were so affectionate and sweet. But it turns out he found them in the middle of Speedway Boulevard dancing in the street. I guess he was kind enough to rescue them and put them each on a leash. And brought them to Jerry, who instantly called animal control to try to locate their owner. They did each have dog tags from two years ago, with license numbers on them. And when I was walking thru to go to the pool, I heard Jerry reading off the license numbers to the person on the other end of the phone.

Before I went into the water, I walked back in to find out the story. And apparently there is a name and address. And everyone is surprised the address of where the dogs live is very far away from where they were found. But Mary, one of the lifeguards, said "maybe the people moved since then." I am sure it will have a happy ending. They are the sweetest most loving dogs in the world. They must have a wonderful home, and the owner will be overjoyed to get them back when Jerry succeeds in locating him.

Two little honey bunnies, lost and on their own. But so sweet, so happy, so trusting, as they were on that guy's long leashes while he was trying to find their home for them. They did not look worried or disturbed. They looked happy as a lark, greeting each newcomer to the pool with all that love and affection and happiness. One would never know to look at them that they had just spent their morning dancing in the middle of Speedway Boulevard, a major traffic artery, and were far from home and lost. They didn't act lost, they acted like two dogs having a ball, where life is just a perfection of joys, joys upon joys upon joys. And love upon love upon love.

Altho if their owner finds out they are not at home safe in his yard, he will be upset. Unless the first he hears about it is from Jerry at the Catalina swimming pool, who is calling him to say "we have your dogs, come pick them up."

Yesterday was day after the election so both Bill and I got down to business. He swept and mopped the whole house before we left for Jerry's pool. And I got a chance to finally write a long email to my mom, and then added a few p.s. emails to that. I also talked to my friend Jan on the phone for an hour, picked up the mail, looked at all the flyers of specials in the stores, emailed my friends again, and even worked on my novel-in-a-month.

I wrote a tiny chapter for it and fixed all the typos. My novel-in-a-month is not going as I planned. At first I had no idea what I would talk about in my novel-in-a-month. I thought I had to have a story, but I didn't know what the story would be. So I described the sky for two hours until a story hit me. Then I decided I would talk about Ruthie's new love, which worked out fabulously. I had a whole first chapter on that, and then the next morning I had another, a tiny chapter on that.

Then I veered off course yesterday to talk about the election and it looks like winter is coming. And then I realized-- how can I go back to talking about Ruthie's new love unless she calls me on the telephone to update me about what is going on now. And since she only calls every 3 weeks, novel-in-a-month will be over before I get the next update.

I told Jan all about it on the phone yesterday, and she said "it is a novel, you are supposed to imagine what happens, invent what happens, make up yourself what happens."

But as I told Jan "I never did that before, I always just write what did happen, I don't make up a thing."

It's really too bad because I did build up nice suspense in my first chapter, and even my second, about what will happen with Ruthie's new love. I think anyone might want to hear what happens next. But maybe I am not a novelist, because unless I get another phone call from Ruthie, I have no idea what happens next.

But I am so enjoying writing my novel-in-a-month, I have no intention of giving it up just because it fizzled out in second chapter. Hahaha I will just keep the pot boiling until I finally do get phone call from Ruthie at end of month, updating me on what has been happening. And so I will have a last chapter to write. Strictly speaking this novel will have a first chapter, and a last chapter, and nothing in between.

Altho the day after Thanksgiving is the big sale on computers. And since Bill must return the computer he borrowed from his friend Jim then, I will have the whole drama of "Bill buys a new computer" as a sub-plot as soon as the day after Thanksgiving arrives.

This is very suspenseful for me, even if it isn't for anyone else, because Office Depot said they won't let anyone know what the new computers on sale will sell for till Thanksgiving morning, when we can all check their website to find out. And of course there is the huge suspense for me of "where the money will come from for this new computer."

I woke up this morning thinking I would call Mary, Bill's younger sister, and see if she wants to chip in for it as Bill's Christmas present. But I realized even what Mary can chip in and what I can chip in, isn't that much, and the best thing is to win the lottery between now and then. I don't have to win the millions and millions that lottery winners win, just a few thousand would put me on easy street, I could afford all the things I want with that.

And of course the week before Thanksgiving Bill and Jim are going to drive up to Phoenix to watch the Cardinals play the Giants in the Cardinals football stadium there. Which is a major event in our life, which has no events, and where nothing ever happens. It will mean leaving early in the morning and going to the airport to rent a car. And then they will have long drive thru beautiful desert. And then a big game in a big stadium. And then long drive home, airport, and then home again. They will get home after midnight.

So I will have a sports chapter in the middle of my novel "Ruthie finds a new love."

Meanwhile I found in yesterday's mail, with all the coupons I did not pick up for a week, a coupon for Anna's Linens, which is in shopping center nearby. And there are comforters on sale and coupon I can use with them. Since I sleep in front of open window and winter nights are sub-freezing, I think I will ask Bill if either before or after pool today, he take me over there. I want to be secure I will be toasty warm on long cold winter nights.

November 7

Ruthie and Soli

This morning I realized in all the ruckus of all the emails sent to and from friends yesterday, there was one thing which was very interesting and which I had totally overlooked.

Apparently Ruthie had been so excited about the election of the new President that she had called up her Egyptian college boyfriend (he is now a government official in charge of antiquities in Egypt) to say "Isn't this great news!" And they had chatted about it. Then he wrote her a long email, and she wrote back a long email to him. And the email I found from her yesterday afternoon when I got back from swimming was about her calling him, and also enclosing the two emails: his to her, and her response.

And apparently he had stayed close friends with everyone he had been close friends with in their left-wing group at Berkeley. He must have been living in America when he went there, because he told Ruthie his mother never went back to Egypt, she continues to live in Cleveland, but he is now a minister of antiquities there.

He is the one who taught Ruthie to be left-wing when she was just a New York liberal when she arrived in college. And then they had gone off to live together in London for a year. He was in a group which was very active in Arabian politics there, and of course he was a major figure in it, and they were all very left-wing.

And then Ruthie came back to New York and joined women's liberation and I met her there. And she said "I have just been living in England for a year with my boyfriend but he was so brilliant and so sure of himself, that gradually I got too intimidated to open up my mouth, I lost confidence in myself."

It was a major love affair tho. He was crazy about Ruthie, she was crazy about him. He adored her, she adored him. And of course it was Ruthie's awakening. He was a revolutionary. He opened her up to that world.

It is why Ruthie was a left-wing activist in the '60s, and why I met her. My dad was a left-wing activist, I had been brought up to that. But Ruthie was introduced to that world by Soli. And it is a world of passion and idealism and activism, and thought and ideas too.

This must have all taken place in college when she was his girlfriend. Because then she was in the same left-wing group he was in and knew all his friends in it, his deepest closest friends, who he has remained friends with to this day.

I think for Ruthie it was an unresolved relationship. On the surface the problem always was (thruout the years, altho they had so little contact thruout the years) "I want him to know I have a mind too, I have ideas too, I want him to respect my mind."

And you know how that never works. You can't communicate your intelligence to someone when you want them to see your intelligence. It just made her more tongue-tied and freeze up.

And on the emotional level, she could never get past the snag "he loved me, I loved him, what went wrong?" And then she would put the two levels together, which turned it into a total mess, because she decided what went wrong is that he didn't respect her.

And then to add torture and confusion to the whole thing, Ruthie's mother got into the act and said "you are not allowed to marry him." She insisted Ruthie give him up. And Ruthie would not defy her mother, and stick up for him. So for all these years she has been mad at her mother for mistreating him, and upset with herself for betraying him, believing she did not have the courage to go thru with it.

And this hornets nest in her mind, until a few weeks ago, when she got a warm confiding email from him about his life, and even asked "any suggestions?" when he described the fork in the road he had come to. And he even said to Ruthie, I haven't told a soul in the world this, I am only telling you. Soli, who has done nothing but politics his whole life, and is at the apex of his career, wants to try something more self-expressive, more feelingful. To open himself up to his own sensitivities and feelings. He wants to chuck his job and become a poet.

Of course as soon as I heard Soli had actually asked for Ruthie's advice, I said "we have to have a long talk with your Higher Self, let her compose the letter back to him, we want her input on advice which would be helpful to him." So Ruthie said OK. And a few weeks ago we got on phone together and tuned into our Higher Selves together, and I asked the questions and Ruthie's Higher Self answered them.

And to our amazement Ruthie's Higher Self explained to both of us the whole story of her relationship with him back then. And nothing was as it seemed to Ruthie during all these past years.

Apparently Soli really had been head over heels in love with Ruthie, was so crazy about her, because of how she was. Exactly because Ruthie was not one of those impressive intellectual girls, expert on politics, but was so warm and alive and fun, that he could express with Ruthie what he could not express with anyone else, not with his friends who were all left-wing stars, nor the women he knew who were so impressive. With Ruthie he could be himself and express his sensitivities and feelings, he could let himself bloom and flower, and be happy.

But the problem was, he kept trying to make Ruthie into one of those other kinds of women, an impressive ideological revolutionary. And according to Ruthie's Higher Self, at the deepest level, Ruthie knew she could not marry him, because she would not marry someone who wanted to make her over into someone she was not.

And so Ruthie deeply confused, upset, and not knowing what the real story was at all, came back to America and he married a woman exactly what he wanted to turn Ruthie into. And apparently it is only now, that the stirring of what Ruthie brought into his life all the way back then, is really demanding release now, even if it costs him his career. He wants to be in contact with those feelings again, he wants to express his sensitivities.

This is what Ruthie's Higher Self explained when we were on the phone together. And why Ruthie's Higher Self encouraged her to write a letter supporting of his finally breaking out. Which Ruthie did.

But mainly that girl was just so happy, so relieved, so at peace, so contented, so deeply pleased with her full heart, to have it all explained to her. In a way where no one was at fault, each had simply acted truly and naturally according to their own heart. Each had simply chosen to be themselves. And yes there had been great love on both sides, which gave so much to both of them, and meant so much to each of them too.

You really have to hand it to our Higher Self, who sees so clearly, understands so well, and realizes yes there was great love, but how can we be unnatural, when we are natural. There is no other choice than the one we made. You can't and won't stifle all the life out of yourself. Our life is who we are, and what we are.

So naturally Ruthie wrote back a loving understanding letter, and said "this is a good thing, you are breaking out and want to enrich your life, and express other sides in it." And he was so grateful and happy to have Ruthie's understanding and approval, for something he thought must be all wrong, but it is what he wants.

And so the first closeness sprang up between them, and they began to communicate and share ideas on all things in email. And after Ruthie's phone call to cheer about the election with him, "Yes my mom in Ohio is out of her mind with joy about it" he wrote in his email. The next thing he told her about was seeing Ted Axelrod. Apparently both Soli and Ted Axelrod were the two luminaries in their left-wing group in college, and best friends. And had kept in touch all these years.

But altho Soli is willing to take his first baby step out of rigid left-wing ideology and that way of seeing the world (he suggested to Ruthie that the reason her letter was so understanding and helpful, because he had heard that she meditated, and there must be something in meditation if she could do that for him). He was not so understanding about Ted Axelrod. Because it appears Sri Govinanda Axelrod visited him in Cairo, and Soli has no sympathy whatsoever for Sri Govinanda Axelrod.

I think he would have been even more disdainful and sarcastic if he wasn't out of his mind with gratitude to Ruthie for being the one person who knows his big change and being supportive of it. He really does think this is a sin to be doing this. Can you imagine his happiness and relief at being told by Ruthie "this is a wonderful thing and cause for celebration." And also he really is kind-hearted and loves so dearly his best friend from college days.

But he is appalled at Sri Govinanda Axelrod. "I guess this is what happens to disillusioned radicals" he wrote to Ruthie yesterday, "they turn into Sri Govinanda Axelrod."

And I guess Ruthie is no longer the scared little mouse afraid to open up her mouth. Because she wrote right back to him, "Well I have been studying Buddhism all these years and you have to admit how brilliant those Buddhists are. And maybe you want to ask Ted what he has learned since he has been on this path, it might be interesting for you to hear...."

Ruthie has stopped trying to come across as still committed Marxist, intellectually adept at left-wing politics, and has decided to let him know who she is now.

And she finished her letter by telling him "my wonderful new boyfriend now, where I am having the best sex I ever had, is also a follower of Yogananda like Ted Axelrod, and I myself went to Muktananda's ashram in India where I had a great experience, and I am having beautiful relationship with my new boyfriend, it is love and respect and freedom."

And so altogether we have a new Ruthie. A circle has been completed. She is open honest revealing and completely loving and understanding with her first boyfriend, who meant so much to her all these years. And has trust and understanding with her new boyfriend who has brought the light of joy and happiness into her life.

November 8

Anne and Alan

Well I overslept big time. I thought the clock must be imagining things when it said 9:30. But then I felt that the air was warm and pleasant so I knew it must be true, because last night was the advent of the BIG COLD. I don't even want to discuss it! I don't even want to think about it! I can't believe it arrived last night and I actually counted the days till it would be gone. It was such a shock for the house to turn ice cold. And I got into bed. There were a lot of covers on it, but not all of them, and I lay there hugging myself for 2 hours trying to get warm.

I guess eventually I will adapt. I will accept that no one can live in this freezing cold and Bill will have to do the stuff which makes it possible for us to have heat. And when sun goes down I will have to shut all the windows and all the doors, and turn on the heat. It doesn't reach my back bedroom anyway, and I won't give up sleeping under open window, so I will pile on all the covers and wear more layers to bed.

But the very first thing I will do, and I will do that today, is put on the flannel sheets and pillow cases. Not only will that warm up my bed a lot, but it will bring in the idea of warmth. LOL I will dress my bed for the weather.

Of course our great beauty arrived yesterday along with winter. It was incredibly breathtakingly beautiful, it really did take your breath away, it really did blow your mind. It was so thrilling to wake up to all that beauty. And at first I said "the cold isn't so bad if this is what it brings." I was just flooded with inspiration and joy yesterday morning about the great beauty.

Today is just as pretty, and because it is now 10 am it is warm and lovely out there. But I had awful time with the cold last night. So even tho it is just as pretty now, what means so much to me is "is it late enough in the morning for the world to have turned warm again?" Until yesterday my number one priority was beauty, now it has slipped to number 2 place. My priority is warmth.

My beautiful swimming pool, the one high up by mountains, closes in a week for whole winter, because of city's decision to save money on heating it. So of course everyone wants to take advantage of it while we still have it. When it is a beautiful day like yesterday it really is a nonpareil there. All the beauty of the day plus the mountains plus that huge wonderful swim pool. It is being in paradise.

I told both Adeena and Samantha about novel-in-a-month because it is not too late for them to start doing it. I had told Samantha, the head lifeguard, about it few days ago and she expressed interest. I emailed her what Lisa had emailed me about it originally, which got me started. But Samantha told me yesterday she hasn't even looked at that email, she has been arriving home at night too exhausted.

She said "what if you are already writing a novel?"

I said "are you writing a novel, Sam?"

"Yes" she said.

"How many pages?" I asked.

"88" she said.

"Well use that then, I am at 44 pages, use what you have" I said, "and then use novel-in-a-month to try to get you to write every day and maybe even finish it, you still can use this thing."

I had no idea if Adeena, a fellow swimmer, is a writer or wanted to write. All I know about Adeena is she grew up in Germany, then married a New Yorker, and the two of them live in Tucson now. She still has strong foreign accent and mainly we have talked about New York, because I have not been back since I moved to Tucson, but Adeena has been back many times to see her husband's family, so she told me all about what it is like now.

I also know Adeena loves to read. She told me she loves to read, but it sounded like biographies and history to me. Bill loves to read history so I introduced them to each other and they had long talk about it.

Bill is now reading history of Civil War, but when I introduced him to Adeena I think he was still reading his history of Ireland, or perhaps that was when he was reading *Rise and Fall of Roman Empire*. I just read Agatha Christie murder mysteries, I don't have the same taste in reading Bill and Adeena have.

Altho when I talked to Adeena about books back then I hadn't discovered I could buy books for 50 cents at the charity store on way home from pool. So my whole life was still TV then.

"What do you like to watch on TV?" I asked Adeena.

"All the live court TV shows" she said.

I have no idea if Adeena ever wrote before or if she just dreams of becoming a writer, but she was definitely interested in novel-in-a-month, far more interested and excited than Samantha.

So I said "leave your email address with Samantha when you go and I will email you what I emailed Sam, everything Lisa sent me about novel-in-a-month; also they have a site where you can register at, it doesn't cost any money, you make up a screen-name, I chose Desert Broom, Sam can choose Calamity Jane, you choose whatever you want; and yesterday they sent out a pep-talk letter to everyone who is registered, encouraging us to go on with our novel, and saying all the advantages to do this."

Lisa and I have been emailing every day. Lisa has never written before, she is doing this all by the book. And the man who began novel-in-a-month 10 years ago even wrote a book about how to do novel in a month. And Lisa bought the book and read it and loved it, and bought a copy for me. I haven't looked at it yet because I figure I already know how to write, I have been doing it long time now.

What is brand new for me in all of this is I never wrote a novel before, never thought I would or could, and I am thrilled down to my toes to be doing it. Lisa did do a great thing for me to get me into this. Plus of course it got me back to my writing which I totally appreciate, who knows when I would have wended my way back there. And it got me to write every single day which I haven't done since I left New York.

In Tucson, even when I am in a writing mode, I take more breaks, I don't just keep on going. I guess my prime happiness is to be writing again, but what intrigues me about all this is the novel thing, that is what makes it all such an interesting new adventure for me.

At first I thought "O goody, I am writing a real novel because I am writing about my friend's love affair." It seemed to me a love affair is the topic of novels. I was reading *Sense and Sensibility* by Jane Austin when I started to write my novel last week. The charity bookstore had 5 Agatha Christies, two by PD James, and *Sense and Sensibility*. I bought all of them. I read all the mysteries first and had started on *Sense and Sensibility* when I was starting my novel, and it was clear the topic of that was the love affairs of the two young sisters.

So naturally when I started my novel last week and was just describing the sky and the weather and what my backyard looked like, hoping an idea for story would come into my mind, when Ruthie's new love affair swam into view, I was ecstatic. "A love affair! Perfect! that is what novels are about! I am writing a novel!"

And I wrote my first chapter and I was so happy. I thought "Great! I have been best friends with Ruthie all these years, I have plenty of material to draw upon, and I can always digress to my own life, this will make a novel." But things didn't work out as I planned. The first chapter is a perfect first chapter to *Ruthie's New Love Affair*. The second chapter wasn't really narrative, it was still on the same topic but mostly observations about it, it was short. And the next morning was the morning after the big election. I woke up with feelings about it. I wasn't interested in Ruthie or her love affair that morning, I wanted to sort out my feelings about losing an election, because here in Tucson my friend lost and I had been deeply involved in that election.

In fact when Lisa first told me about novel-in-a-month, at first I wasn't interested, then I thought I would do it, but I had decided I would start on November 5th. As I told Lisa "I will start after the election because my whole mind will be on the election beforehand."

But it turned out I started the day before the election. The morning of the election I was writing about Ruthie's new love affair. I had actually put the election out of my mind the day before when I started writing it; and the morning of it, I was happy writing my novel.

But the day after the election, when I had to lick my wounds, that was the only thing in my mind when I woke up. I had a loss, how to go on from here. What else could I write about! I wanted to resolve it in my mind and writing seemed like the best way to do it. And so I decided to see it as a change and change is a good thing. Even if it was not what I wanted, it would bring in unexpected benefits, because that is the nature of change.

So then I was at peace about it. Altho I knew I had gone off course in my novel, I wondered what would happen the next day. And the next day I didn't go back to Ruthie or her love affair either. And this time I had no excuse. It just wasn't where my head was at, what I was in the mood to write about. I just felt like writing about my yesterday, which I did.

But of course I was dismayed that my novel had fizzled out. I thought "O well, a first chapter about Ruthie's love affair, a last chapter about Ruthie's love affair, and every chapter in between will be about how I spent my yesterday."

I still loved that it was a novel, and that I was calling it a novel, I loved it that I was involved with a project where there was a whole, that I could see this all as a whole. But I did feel in my heart of hearts this wasn't really a novel.

I guess in my mind a short story, which is what I always write, the whole story takes place in that story. Whereas a novel, the whole story takes place in a novel, it is a much bigger story, bigger in size, because it takes up a whole novel.

I said to myself "but *Sense and Sensibility* isn't only about the sisters' love affairs, she has everything under the sun in there." But it didn't work to convince me, because her novel is "and then, and then, and then." Each chapter begins off with "and then" and tells what happens then. Which is just the way I write a story, which is how any story goes. A story is just "and then, and then, and then." It wasn't just about the sisters' love affairs, it was everything which happened in their lives during that 5 month period.

So I accepted my novel was not going to be one big story like the one I was reading, where I was so curious to read what happened next. There wasn't going to be any "next" in my novel, it was just going to be about how I spent my November, just putting bookends around a little time in my life, which was fine with me. Altho I was wistful that what had excited me when I started, a bona fide novel story, wasn't going to happen and it was going to be same old thing.

And then suddenly out of the blue yesterday it wasn't same old thing. Because a little tiny thing, buried deep in an email Ruthie sent me, suddenly swam into view.

There had been a lot of emails that day, the day before yesterday. Even tho novel-in-a-month site said "you can't show your writing to anyone here, you can only post your word count, and go on chat rooms and discuss what you are doing, no one can see your novel till the end." And so Lisa and I were not showing each other what we were writing, we were just saying our word count to each other, and how it was going, and our experience of it. I decided to send out my first 4 chapters to a few friends, I wanted to share what I had written.

And when I told Lisa on email "I have gone off course and am just writing my yesterday again and I don't know if I will ever get back on course," she wrote back "why would you do that, this is your opportunity to write a novel, why write what you have always written when you can do something new." And so I decided to send what I wrote to Lisa too.

But yesterday morning I remembered the tiny little thing at the bottom of the email Ruthie sent me. It was an email about her calling her college boyfriend, and the email he sent her, and the one she wrote back. And it was something buried in his email, which gave me an idea.

So yesterday I wrote about him and Ruthie, their relationship. Because the boyfriend you live with during college and after college and who you plan to marry, and who is the one who started your awakening, is a major relationship.

For me it came to a natural end. I moved out, he was upset, but we stayed very close till Bill moved in with me, and Rosie moved in with him, and we have been best friends forever.

We lost contact 8 years ago, but I called him last winter and it was a beautiful phone call. We were both lost in the glory of what we each had brought the other back then. I was so appreciative of what he had brought into my life back then at 21, and he was so appreciative of what I had brought into his.

And we had helped each other over the years when we were close friends too. We were both writers. Altho Alan was writing his book on Marxism, I was writing short stories. But after Ruthie got me on computer, and I saw what God's gift that was to writers, I got Alan on the computer and boy he sure appreciated it too.

As soon as he finished his book on Marxism and the labor movement, a real book company wanted to publish it. They assumed he was a professor and wrote him a letter, "Dear Dr Cantos." I couldn't believe that Alan wrote scholarly text on Marx and Engels and the labor movement, and publishers snapped it up. Whereas I was writing all my wonderful short stories and no publisher would go near it with a ten foot pole.

But a peculiar thing happened. Naturally Alan's book had about a million quotes by Marx, and his publisher insisted he get permission for them before they could publish his book. And it turned out World Publishers, a small outfit on 14th Street of leftists, owned all the rights to those quotes. And when Alan called up Mrs. Appelbaum, as a formality, to ask for permission to use all the quotes, she said no. She said "if you want to use the quotes you have to pay us $1000 for each quote," and since there were about a million quotes that was impossible.

Alan called his big brother who had a rage, and said "take her to court! take her to court! that is outrageous!" Alan's big brother was furious at her. But in the story Alan told me about the upsetting phone call with Mrs. Appelbaum, buried way down in the story, as just a minor detail, Mrs. Appelbaum had said "why didn't you take your book to us first!"

And suddenly I understood everything. Mrs. Appelbaum was being recalcitrant and difficult because she was envious Academic Press was going to publish it. She wanted the book, she wanted to publish it, and she was insulted Alan had not brought it to her.

"Alan!" I said, "you bought all those beautiful new clothes and you look so good in them. Just take Mrs. Appelbaum out to lunch. Take her to a beautiful fancy restaurant. You are so good at that, and can be so charming and classy. She is mad because she wants to publish your book and you didn't offer it to her. All you have to do is take her out to lunch, dress beautifully, be absolutely lovely to her, and promise her your next book you will bring right to her."

I don't know if Alan believed me, but it was a solution he was willing to try. He wrote Mrs. Appelbaum a long lovely letter, telling her just how much the books from World Publishers have meant to him. There were enough compliments in that letter to her publishing company, and to her, to make her head spin.

I don't know if he ever did take her to lunch. Because when she called Alan back, butter couldn't melt in her mouth. She insisted she have the rights to the paperback edition of the book, which of course put Alan in 7th heaven. He never dreamed anyone would want to put it out in paperback, he was thrilled. And she graciously let him have all the quotes by Marx and Engels for free. And they are the best of friends. And he promised Mrs. Appelbaum, as soon as he finishes his next book he will bring it right to her. And she was gratified, and so was Alan. He already had a publisher lined up for his next book.

If Alan had held any grievance against me for breaking up with him 20 years before, I bet that made up for it. I had turned that whole situation around for him. Instead of now being impossible to get his book published, that was coming out, he was already preparing the paperback edition with Mrs. Appelbaum, and he had a publisher lined up for his next book.

And I had the gratification of seeing spirituality really did pay off. I had just started to be spiritual at that time, and I knew having a rage and going to war was not the best solution. It was the one Alan's big brother suggested, but I had learned differently. Instead of seeing Mrs. Appelbaum as a monster, there was another way to look at it, and I was able to find it when I looked for it. It gratified me and reinforced my belief in spirituality, that it was so practical, that I could use it to help my friend Alan get everything he wanted.

Alan had been very insulting when I first started on this path. It had began with me praying, with me believing in God, and reading the Gospel of St John to find words of comfort for the terrible travails I was going thru then. I don't know how Alan knew I was reading the Gospel of St John. Did I confide it to him? or did he see the open book in my kitchen?

All I know is he said, "this is awful Anne, you are like one of the crazy women you see in the subway, who are always reading the Bible and talking to themselves."

I was so happy to be able to help Alan, that I did not mention to him "I am not a crazy lady on the subway after all."

I took a lot of flack from a lot of people when I first started on my spiritual path. They just didn't understand. But I was really lucky too in the companionship and encouragement I did receive from friends.

Ruthie started me off on it, she became spiritual first, and when she said "prayer works" at a moment when I was desperate out of my mind, I tried it and it did work. And she did talk about God and Jesus and New Testament to me, which was very radical for me back then. Because Ruthie was a Jewish girl and I was a Jewish girl, and I thought Jesus was taboo for Jews. She did succeed in taking off that taboo for me, but the path she wound up on was different path. Going to Guru Muktananda's ashram in India had meant a lot to her, and she had become a follower of his. And the path she wound up on was Buddhism. She studied all the Buddhist Texts and went to see the Dalai Lama whenever she could.

It was just the grace of the Universe, when I was having such a terrible time and was in such desperate need for help, that that was the time Ruthie said "prayer works." And that was the time she was having her experience with the New Testament and Jesus. Before that it had been Guru Muktananda, and after that it was only Buddhism. But where she was at that moment turned out to be the start of the path for me.

Because my path was prayer, Gospel of St John, then *A Course In Miracles*. My path was one straight line. I was not an explorer in all the realms of spirituality like Ruthie. She was more like a butterfly, delighting in each beautiful flower, or like a bee gathering honey from all the flowers in the field. She used meditation to calm her down, and then used spirituality as a great exploration and adventure. She got real and meaningful experiences wherever she went in this spiritual adventure, and loved studying her Buddhist texts, and going to lectures by Lamas and learning from them and connecting to them.

For me everything was simple, direct, practical, and taking place during the most stressful of times. All I ever wanted was comfort, all I ever wanted was peace, and all I ever wanted was to save my marriage, and to save the lives of my pets.

I prayed, I read the Gospel of St John, I got in touch with my Higher Self, and I read *A Course In Miracles*. Finally a few months before I moved to Tucson, during one of those intensely stressful times, I made a higher firmer connection with my Higher Self and decided to stay there. I just decided to give over direction of my life to my Higher Self, and to always be in touch with her love, her practical suggestions, and her reassurance, and of course her great understanding offered to me whenever I wanted it.

So you could say my spiritual path was fast and direct (altho I wish it on no one, going thru hell is not my idea of fun). I went from prayer to Gospel of St John to my Higher Self. Incredible bouts of stress made me move each step, and hahaha each time I was ready to slack off and fall back, a new bout of incredible stress would arrive to keep me marching forward.

I was pushed along like a hurricane at my back. And I would sum up the whole experience as being like in a terrifying hurricane for a long time. Altho of course if that is the spiritual path you choose (and obviously I did, altho where and how I did I have no idea) it has to be a crash course, no one can live that way forever.

Ruthie delighted in going to see Guru Muktananda when he was up in the Catskills, delighted in going to EST 10 years before it even occurred to me spirituality exists. And to this day she takes so much pleasure in seeing the Lamas when they come to San Diego.

Hers has been such a long delightful adventure. Mine was not! But whereas mine brought me right to my Higher Self, which was (I guess) its destination from the get-go (it is the only thing which would make sense of everything, makes it clear path to that single destination). Ya know I don't think Ruthie's path has a destination, it really is the butterflies and honey bees delighting in their meadow, Ruthie's path is delight.

But what is so interesting is that no one has to go thru what I went thru to arrive at their Higher Self. For some it just arrives on their own. When Bill became a painter in Tucson (went thru art school, had finished art school, and was now on his own about painting) and was now stymied and couldn't get thru, couldn't figure out how to move forward, he would sleep on that couch under Irene's big abstract painting, and every night before he fell asleep, his dilemma was always in his mind.

He couldn't find a way out of it. And then one night he heard a voice saying to him in his own head, "you are learning, just treat it as learning experience, you don't have to paint a masterpiece, just try to learn, treat it all as practice."

And this was the solution for Bill. He has adopted this attitude and it has worked ever since. "It is just practice" he says when he starts a painting, "I just want to learn." But I knew what that voice was, and who that voice was. And I showed Bill how he could ask it any question on any topic and get help from it.

Like everyone, like me too, when we first connect to our Higher Self, we use it to solve that problem at hand. It solves it for us, we are so relieved, and then go back to our regular life and regular voice in our mind. It takes a long time for anyone, me included, to develop the habit and choose the habit of consulting our Higher Self on everything.

November 10

Cold misty air

Well I am more peaceful about winter and enjoying it more now that it moderated itself for the past 2 days. The huge wind kept the cold from coming down last night, the warm air stayed. I was too warm sleeping in my pullover, and finally I just took it off.

And when I woke up in the middle of the night I walked in just my skirt and topless out one back door and in the kitchen backdoor, to find a little shift to put on. It was fun being half naked in the night winter air. And it was not wintry; chilly but not cold. I didn't really need all those covers I slept under and tried to throw them off as I slept.

And right now the air coming in from my open window all over me, I'd kind of describe it as a cold mist, but refreshing and not too cold. It's mist because there is cloud cover, this is damp air but I don't care, it is fresh cold damp. But it must be just the right temperature to make the world feel frosty delicious without being too chilly for comfort. I am in long sleeves now of course and it is a warm pullover, but my body is still all warm and toasted from night's sleep.

Bill got up before me and put the coffee up before me. And now he is sitting in a spot in the yard where I can see him thru my open window. The sun has not yet reached the picnic table and chairs, it is just in that one corner, so he is sitting in that one corner having toast and coffee. Wearing a baseball hat with hooded sweatshirt, and hood over the baseball cap, and sweatpants and sneakers without socks.

I am watching him eat his toast and drink his coffee. He just finished his toast and rubbed his hands together. O now he is picking up his coffee cup and looking around. Now he picked up the plate the toast was on and is heading towards the house.

I can see my two down comforters on the clothesline at the back of yard. I have had them both long time, and one is so dingy colored now it's impossible to know it was ever white. The other one I must have bought more recently, you can see that it is white, altho nothing like the snowy pristine white when I got it. It might be the off-white people paint their houses, or what happens to white walls as time goes by.

I guess they had both slipped off my bed at the end of last winter, so for past 6 months my dog Beanie has been making it his bed. He likes sleeping next to me, he only spends part of the night actually on my bed sleeping with me, but he likes his lair next to my bed. And sure enough I found a lot of dog cookies under the two comforters, when I decided to take them to the clothesline yesterday to freshen them up.

I did buy two down comforters at Anna's Linens few days ago, which I thought would see me thru the winter, but when I opened them up when I got home, I found out why the price was so reasonable. They are very thin, and what made the package so heavy was that two pillows were included with it. I think with all the blankets and comforters I have on my bed now (altho I gave one of those new ones to Bill) I would be fine if it went down to the 40s, I would not freeze, but it is not warm enough for the 20s and low 30s. And I can't afford to buy any more bedding.

I had never planned to use those two old dingy comforters that the doggie slept on for past 6 months as part of my bedding this winter. I thought those comforters had really had it. But yesterday I decided to put them on the line and let the winds blow thru them, that that would freshen them up, and I would buy a comforter cover.

I got the idea of comforter covers when I was in Anna's Linens. She showed me the down comforters she had and said "it only comes in white, but here are the duvet covers for it, it is 30 dollars." It never occurred to me to spend 30 dollars so white comforter would stay pristine white. But it seemed a very good idea for two very old comforters, extremely dingy, which the dog had slept on since last winter.

If you are decided to use the dog's bed this winter, at the very least you want to put it in a pretty new comforter cover, otherwise the sight of it would be too awful. They really were an awful sight when I dug them out from under the dog's bed, and with dog cookies all over. But I resolutely brought them out to the line yesterday before the sun went down, and they actually seemed in good shape. Not good looking, but serviceable comforters. They were in better shape than they looked crushed down at the bottom of the dog's bed.

I so rarely go into my yard anymore, except to go to picnic table to have lunch or to sun-couch to bathe in the beautiful sunshine. But here I was in the back near the fence where the clothesline was, hour before sunset in my own yard. And I tell you my yard seemed absolutely wonderful to me. It doesn't look like much when I look at it out my own window while I type. We have just let it go desert. I used to spend a lot more time in it when we first moved here and Bill planted all those wonderful plants. I would go out in the evening and water them all.

Now it is just scruffy backyard, with big tree in the center, a huge mesquite tree, and various mesquite trees sprang up in other places in the yard. And I have no idea why, when I was at the very back, trying to figure out how to get the comforters on the clothes line, I looked around and thought "this is paradise." I had no idea I had such a wonderful backyard. I understood why my doggie loves it so much. And I really don't know why I thought "this is paradise," why I felt like I was in a paradise.

Maybe because it is an hour before sunset, and there was so much beauty from all the shadows coming in. Maybe it was a peaceful time. Maybe because unbeknownst to me, a storm was going to blow in from the mountains in an hour or two. Or maybe it was just the spaciousness, and freshness of being among the plants, out in the plant world.

You know I think that is it. Suddenly I had a full experience of being in the plant world. Way in the back of yard where I never go, where no one goes but Beanie, or very occasionally Bill to pin up his laundry, is really a lovely undisturbed plant world, a happy plant world. And I was in the midst of it, and I knew this is paradise. Plants must really really really be wonderful, if they are the experience of paradise. And I was in their world and I loved it.

My clothesline I discovered is in terrible shape. But there were clothespins on it and I did manage to pin up both comforters. It's so odd that I had been vaguely dreading it, or not looking forward to it all, digging up the old comforters from the dog's bed and taking them out to the clothesline. But it turned out I loved it. It was thrilling to discover I live in paradise even if I don't know it or go there. And to be in it too.

So I pinned up both comforters. And after that the huge winds came in and blew and blew and blew, and I thought this is good for freshing my comforters. And later when night came and I was in bed reading Agatha Christie, to my huge surprise, I saw all kinds of lightning light up above the mountains. It didn't make a sound so I thought I imagined it at first. It seemed thrilling to me. This soundless lightning over the mountains.

"Lightning over the mountains" I said to myself, it sounded so Chinese, like one of the things you get when you do the *I Ching*. I forget what they are called now, you throw the pennies 6 times to make your hexagram, and then you look up what you got, and could get "Lightning over the mountains." O that's why! because each hexagram has a name, and the name is always two elements of nature put together, and I got lightning over the mountains.

It came out of nowhere and was soundless. And was diffused white light from the clouds, like lightning above the clouds. It was pretty, and spectral, so dreamlike, because it was so subtle. If you hadn't happened to be looking in exactly that direction you would not even know it was happening.

And because it had nothing to do with the natural rhythm of storms (all that building and releasing itself in a storm), just something which happened out of nowhere, I had the oddest feeling that this has to be now, that it means something.

I can't explain what I mean. It was as if you had been feeling as if we are in time of transformation, that you and the whole Planet, and the whole sh-bang, were going thru a transformation, that something was really happening, and that something very brand new and different were coming in.

And then you looked up and saw all these lightning over mountains, and so it seemed like a comment or an omen or a prophecy. You looked at it and thought "of course, I know what it is." It was reinforcement of what I had been feeling, like a tangible seeing of it. As if all my feelings about how things were, suddenly manifested in this silent lightning over the mountains.

Then I heard the thunder and Beanie got alarmed, and so I wanted it to stop so my Beanie would not be alarmed. And I got up and shut off both computers, the one Bill's friend Jim lent him, and mine, because I thought if there is lightning all over the sky I want my computers to be safe. Bill said "you don't have to, it is far away and not coming here," and I knew he was right but I still did it.

He was watching the football game in his room. The instant he had gotten back from the movies, Priscilla had appeared. She is the outdoors kitty who comes to Bill whenever he is home, meowing for her food. It all happened so fast. I had just gone into my other room to lie in bed and read Agatha Christie when Bill returned home from the movies. He looked in and said "hi" and said "I'm going in to watch the game."

"OK" I said, "I won't get up then, so Beanie will stay here with me, because Priscilla will try to find you for her food."

Just at that instant I saw the lightning over the mountains for the first time, and called out to Bill "I saw lightning over the mountains." That was when I thought I imagined it.

But Bill said "I know, I saw it while I was driving home."

And then the next thing I knew Bill called out "Priscilla had her supper." She must have found him in an instant. How she knows the exact instant he gets back from the movies I have no idea.

Priscilla and Bill have a whole life together that I know nothing about. Because I am always abjured to keep Beanie away when Bill is around the house. Beanie won't leave my side, so whichever room I am in, I don't get up and move about at all when Bill goes into the kitchen. Because that is when Priscilla finds him.

Priscilla will actually spend her whole time with Bill as long as Beanie and I are nowhere to be seen. Altho when Beanie does appear, she skedaddles out of house with Beanie hard on her heels.

I don't see why I have to be lumped with the ogre. I would like to see Priscilla too. But the way it is Bill and Priscilla have whole life together, are getting to know each other and are close, and I am always with Beanie in a far distant room. I am not allowed to get up and move about the house while Priscilla is having her dinner. And Priscilla likes being served 6 times a day. As Bill said "I don't know where she puts it all."

November 11

Ruthie Tunes into her Higher Self

It was a Thursday afternoon, maybe a year ago, I was thinking about Ruthie's palmistry video. I remember I was at my picnic table in backyard. I wasn't doing anything. I don't remember what I was eating or drinking. I might have just been sitting there to be in the sunshine. But I was definitely thinking about Ruthie's palmistry video.

Apparently in San Diego-- even tho in NYC she had a very good job for Adelphi University, her job was anyone who had a problem with computer, Ruthie helped them with it, and anyone who wasn't already on the computer she taught them how to go on. She had been my computer teacher-- arranged for me to be bought a computer and then taught me how to use it for my writing, so I know what a good teacher Ruthie is and what a good teacher of computer.

And what she did for me she did for everyone at Adelphi, plus helped them with more advanced things if they wanted that, since all I did on computer was word process. I am sure when email and internet came along Ruthie taught them how to do that, which she also did for me.

A month after she moved to San Diego, she called me up and said "it is time for you to be on email and internet" and taught me how on the phone and I have been on email and internet ever since. And of course I had been wanting that but hadn't known how to do it. And a year later when I got the worst virus in the world on my computer because I had no protection, she sat on the phone with me for almost 6 hours to get rid of it. It was a huge job. Ruthie is a saint to do that for me. And she does it for anyone and everyone. She loves to help.

In San Diego at first she offered her services as a free-lancer to help anyone with computer. But that did not take off. What did take off, to her huge surprise, is-- Ruthie's mother could do palm reading, and had done it her whole life and taught Ruthie. And Ruthie would do it for her friends, just as a hobby, she is very psychic.

How it began in San Diego, I don't know. Maybe she sat in front of supermarket with a little stand, and sign which read "Palms read, $5." Whatever it was, people loved her reading so much, they invited her to their parties to read the palms of their guests, and she got paid quite a pretty penny for this.

And then people who got reading from Ruthie, liked it so much they recommended her to their friends. And eventually Ruthie had a growing flourishing business as a psychic palm reader, which she still does. She has new clients all the time. She is invited to read palms at parties at the big hotels there.

And when her son graduated high school there, she was invited to read the palms of all the graduates, and could tell each and every one of them how wonderful they are, and all the amazing talents and abilities they have. It was an inspired idea to hire Ruthie to read the palms of all the new high school graduates, to be able to see themselves and their future in such glowing colors.

And I guess she also taught palmistry classes there, taught others how to read palms. And one day she decided to video her teaching of a palmistry class. I guess a palmistry class, Ruthie talks about the history of palm reading, which is actually very interesting. I watched her video and I learned about it. Then she teaches about it, and then she reads the palm of everyone in her class.

Her video was very short tho. It is just the first part, where she tells them all about the history of palm reading. And she liked it, and wanted to edit it. And apparently, a woman friend of Ruthie, this was the time when she was finally making friends in San Diego--

Ruthie in San Diego, like me in Tucson, when we first moved here, there was a long time before we made any friends. We both had had gazillion friends back in New York and it was so surprising and unusual to be living in a place with no friends at all.

Altho I can recognize now, altho it was difficult then, what a necessary and lovely phase this really is in our relocation. The long time with no socializing at all, really does clear your mind from all the over-socializing back in New York. Because you aren't making any new friends, and have limited telephone time with your old friends, all you can really do is think about your old friends. And eventually there is no more to think about. And a vacancy comes into your mind, you are bored.

And it is during this vacancy and boredom, that new interests come into your mind. I got interested in news and politics on TV and eventually became an internet poster on political forums.

And that is when Ruthie became a palmist in San Diego. Holding their hand and telling them all about themselves, probably brought the communication back into her life, that she loved. It was a nice balance. You get to socialize and be intimate and communicate and share love and ideas, but it is structured, it doesn't turn into emotional complicated relationship where you fight and get upset.

And maybe posting on the internet did the same for me. I got to enjoy communication, friendship, conviviality, sharing of ideas and perception, and still have a quiet peaceful life. It solved the problem of having no friends in Tucson, plus I got to share my new interests with others who were interested in the same thing.

And so when the time came to start making friends in real life in Tucson, it could happen as naturally and gradually, as friendships always happen in our life, the pressure was off.

And so Ruthie must have started having friends there, if Ruthie mentioned to a woman "I did my video but I don't know how to edit it."

And she offered-- she said "my husband is a video expert, let him edit your video for you."

It had been a big thing for Ruthie about editing her video. She had done it, made the video, but she couldn't move forward till she edited it, and she didn't know how. So she was always procrastinating, and she wanted it to be completed of course. So she was immensely grateful.

And right away things went wrong. I don't remember if they lost her video when Ruthie first gave it to them, something like that. So she got another one and gave it to them. And basically what happened is her husband, the video expert, instead of editing Ruthie's video and handing it back to her as a video which is now complete, the reverse happened. He told Ruthie all the things which were wrong with her video, and by the time he finished, Ruthie was hopeless. She wanted to give up on her video and had no confidence in herself or her video.

And I must have just had this conversation with her the day before (heard the whole story) when I walked out into the sunshine that Thursday afternoon to think about it and talk it all over with my Higher Self, because I thought it wasn't fair what happened to Ruthie, and I wanted my Higher Self to make it up to her.

And what seemed so logical to me, sitting in the sunshine, was if Ruthie couldn't edit her video herself, and if the video expert had just made her lose heart for her video, then the solution was for Ruthie to tune into her Higher Self, and let her Higher Self tell her exactly how to edit her video. Her Higher Self knows how to do this. Let her Higher Self be her editor.

So my Higher Self said "Great idea! Go in and call Ruthie now and teach her how to tune into her Higher Self."

I liked the idea very much because it turned what had been a big loss into a huge gain. She had had such a bad experience with the video expert, but as a result she would get her Higher Self. Ruthie had never expressed the slightest interest in tuning into her Higher Self, even tho she knew I did, but I didn't see that as an obstacle. I figured if my Higher Self said "Great! go ahead and do it now!" Ruthie would be receptive.

And I am sure my voice was a little different when I called her, because tuning into your Higher Self is all about being quiet. I wasn't weird or anything, but I was not loud excited stimulating, I was quiet, and friendly.

"Hi Ruthie" I said, "what are you doing now?"

She said "nothing, I am sitting here doing nothing."

"Good" I said. "It is very unfair your friend's husband ruined your video for you, so I thought maybe you would like your Higher Self to edit it for you. She will do a great job and it will be easy. I can teach you how to tune into Her right now. It is very easy, and doesn't take any time."

"I'm game," Ruthie said.

"Good," I said.

And it took about 30 seconds and Ruthie was hearing her own Higher Self in her mind. And so I asked questions and Ruthie's Higher Self answered them and Ruthie said all the answers out loud as she heard them.

Apparently Ruthie had been feeling sad when I called her, and after we were launched getting answers from her Higher Self, her Higher Self said "Ruthie is crying now." I guess hearing that loving understanding voice in her mind, let all her feelings come to the surface and break thru.

So her Higher Self suggested she go into her back yard and find an avocado for her lunch, and also to get her camera and take pictures of what it looked like after the rain there. We were on the phone the whole time with her Higher Self as Ruthie was moving around and doing this. I guess when Ruthie started to cry, her Higher Self thought the best thing for Ruthie was to be moving and doing something to distract herself.

What a strange afternoon that was! Because Ruthie needed batteries for her camera to work, so Ruthie, me, and her Higher Self drove to Costco, bought the batteries, went into the backyard, took all the photos. And then Ruthie was relaxed and happy to have long talk with her Higher Self. I still asked all the questions. I wanted Ruthie to see how her Higher Self could give her information on any topic under the sun.

And I thought a topic which would interest Ruthie would be all her old boyfriends, to hear what her Higher Self had to say about all those relationships, what she had offered the boy, and what the boy had offered her. Plus it is a way to see all the people involved, and Ruthie herself, with such peaceful loving eyes.

It was a long day. But I figured Ruthie had enough practice now tuning into her Higher Self and hearing her Higher Self, that now she could do it on her own, she didn't need me anymore. She could do it whenever she wanted to.

And then of course I was sure she did ask questions about her son, her son is her whole life, and so Ruthie would want to consult with such a voice of wisdom, about how to see things and how to act which would be most helpful to him. Any mother would.

And a few days later Ruthie called and said, "I found a list of all the big problems in my life, that I wanted to ask the Lama from Tibet about when he visited San Diego next week, and I realized they are all solved now, my Higher Self solved each and every one of them, they are no longer problems for me." And I thought "good, she sees how helpful her Higher Self is."

But then like everyone who tuned into their Higher Self for the first time-- it was the same with me, unless there is an emergency in our life, we forget all about our Higher Self, but a month or two later her friend came to spend Christmas vacation in San Diego.

And at first Ruthie spent all her time at the hotel with her friend, but then her friend decided to stay in San Diego, and how it was hard for Ruthie, because of course she wanted to be home with her son too, and she was being pulled in two directions. And so she spent that whole time with her Higher Self, having help so she could be fair to everyone and fair to herself, and not get swept away.

It is very helpful to have our Higher Self available to us every instant when we are in the midst of situation we don't know how to manage, because She knows how to manage it so beautifully.

And then after that there was no question her Higher Self was solid source of help if she ever cared to avail herself of it. But again, like everyone else, she totally forgot about her Higher Self. No one remembers unless they are at the end of their rope. And altho Ruthie's life had ups and downs, and stress did come into it, there was never the kind of suffering where someone who has forgotten their Higher Self would want to remember.

So it would only be when we happened to be chatting on the phone, and Ruthie happened to be recounting a situation where she had conflicts, or wasn't sure how to deal with it, that I would say "why don't we do Higher Self? ask for her input?" And Ruthie would say "fine."

And she would tune in and I would ask questions. And it was always interesting, gratifying, and informative, we both learned a lot. Because Ruthie did not have a dire problem, so after coming up with solutions for all of

Ruthie's immediate problems, her Higher Self would explain to both of us what is taking place now on the Planet, why we are having the experiences in our lives now we are having and what they mean.

It was very nice, like being two sisters with a mother, and she would talk about Ruthie and talk about me. She even told Ruthie "Anne has a destination, she is climbing a mountain, whereas you make networks between people, you bring people together."

And I got off the phone and found it very interesting to have heard "Anne has a destination, she is climbing a mountain."

We did not talk about me very much with her Higher Self, but Ruthie's instinct is so inclusive that as much as she was starving to hear all about her, always towards the end she would ask about Anne. Altho since I was the one asking the questions and I never asked about myself, her Higher Self must have known that was in Ruthie's mind, that Ruthie wanted her to talk about Anne too so Anne would be included, so Ruthie could express her generosity, that there be something for Anne in all this too. Her Higher Self would know that is balance Ruthie would want.

And that is where we are now. We have done it together maybe 8 times over the past year, it could be less, 5 times. But each time it was wonderful. It is just so nice to have the Voice of Wisdom explain it all to both of us. And Ruthie and I are both so appreciative of what we hear and never could have known that.

And afterwards when we finish "the session" Ruthie and I chat for few minutes about what we just heard, but there isn't that much to say, we just say which was the most interesting part. I think what makes it amazing is we heard it together. There is something about this whole experience (that our hearts beat as one all thru it and about it) and that is an unusual thing to share with a friend.

I don't remember now what Ruthie's Higher Self said about her first boyfriend, Theodore, or about Soli. I remember what She said about Al because I know Al and knew them as boyfriend and girlfriend. She said "what Al gave Ruthie was delight, and what Ruthie gave Al was delight." And she said "Roberto was her soul mate or very close to a soul mate." That was her realest and closest relationship.

And about me, this was in a much later phone call, she said "Anne is like a leaf at the very end of a branch of a tree now, but Ruthie is at the part of the tree where most people are. Which makes it perfect. Because when Anne discovers things, it wouldn't mean anything to anyone. But she can tell Ruthie, and that way it goes out to all. Because Ruthie is where people are and she communicates."

Hahaha Ruthie is like a central switchboard. I like to be out there and see things but what I can see it turns out I can't communicate in a way anyone could understand. But Ruthie does. And thru her central switchboard anyone who wants to see what I see can see it thru her. A tree is a very good metaphor for all this, because we are all part of the same tree, and each performing the function of a tree we love to do best. Of course I would love to be a leaf at the farther end of branch, just open to wind currents and blue sky and sun, floating in the breeze, with my sparrows as my companions.

And Ruthie apparently is connected to all people, connection is her thing, she loves to connect and is so good at it. And so Ruthie brings all the connections to me, and what the breezes whisper to me goes thru Ruthie and all thru the tree.

Ruthie makes everything accessible to all. That is why she was the one who started me on my spiritual path, she was already well along on hers and had learned a lot. But what she communicated at her 40th birthday party to all of us who were there, I was able to use to help me in my life and that is what started my own spiritual path.

And now I am a leaf on a branch and Ruthie is another place doing another thing, making everything accessible to all.

And even tho I think "Wouldn't Ruthie want to be leaf on branch like me?" and Ruthie may think "Wouldn't Anne want to be doing what I am doing?" It is the same as when we sat around on the floor of tenement apartments in the '60s, with the lights out and candles lit, and incense lit, smoking pot, and felt so sorry for our parents that they were not doing the same thing.

"If only our parents could have this too" we all said, it was the only fly in the ointment of our perfect happiness. We didn't stop longing for our parents to have this too, till Janet sensibly said "but maybe it would not make them happy."

November 12

Busy Day

Yesterday was a huge day, I don't know how I did it, I would not want to do it again.

O well let me try to describe my day. That is the only way I can begin to understand it. It began off so ordinary like every other day. I have such a dreamy simple empty life, but that was not my yesterday. I did not meander dreamily thru my day. It was like 4th of July celebration, made out of firecrackers. And one thing followed another in quick succession.

It began off ordinary it seems to me (altho who can remember yesterday, so much happened, yesterday morning seems like an eternity ago now). Altho for other people this could be a normal day, it was just a busy day, nothing out of the ordinary happened. It is just that busy-ness is something, like a few grains of salt on slice tomato, I am used to busy-ness being the flavor in a day, not a whole day of it.

Hahaha I was busy all day.

I had my regular morning. The busy-ness did not begin till I got back from the pool. We went to the pool and it was closed for Veterans Day, so we just came home and that is when I began my busy day. And it didn't end till 10 o'clock and I had not even read my *Letter From God* for that day. And when I tried to read it, I could not, my mind was too busy.

It began off like every other regular day. Bill and I woke up at same time, and we both overslept. For some reason these past nights, I am up for long time in middle of night. I wake up several times, and am up long time, and then when I do finally fall asleep, I oversleep. Which is fine, because we are in winter now, to wake up at 5 am would not be good, it is too cold and too dark. I would be freezing in my computer room. Better to be nestled under all my down covers, warm and toasty in my nest. And wake up to blue sky and sunshine, and the start of warmth.

Bill might have liked to talk to me when we were both first up in kitchen making our coffee. He might even have been the one who put up the coffee. But I got out the half-

and-half for us to have with it, and variety of pastries if anyone wanted one. I said "I am going to go in and work on my novel, wish me luck." And he said "OK, I won't talk to you then."

And it's possible I might have wanted to describe the beauty of the day, and where I was right now in the middle of my life. But I was strongly urged to write about Ruthie tuning into her Higher Self, to tell the story of how I taught Ruthie to tune into her Higher Self, and about that shared experience.

If I wasn't writing a novel, if it was just one of my stories, even if I were going to write about that, I would set it up so differently. I would move from the middle of the moment now to it. That is the big difference for me in writing a novel. In all my stories I begin right in the middle of the moment now. I like to begin in now-ness, no matter where I go to or end up. For me life always begins in the now. But of course I never wind up where I think I will go. Starting in the now can lead anywhere. And I am like *row row row your boat merrily down the stream,* I just follow the stream where it goes.

But a novel is something else. I am seeing you don't have to create now-ness each time you start. It does not have to be absolutely fresh like that. Hahaha you can have a plan and plod along on your plan. You don't have to take that leap into the unknown each time you start. You can just say "this is what I was talking about in the chapter two days ago, and I never got to finish it, so I will talk about it now."

And that is what I did yesterday morning. It wasn't actually two days ago that I didn't get to finish, it was Saturday. And for some reason Saturday we both woke up so late, and I was writing so much in that story, that even tho at some point in it I knew I wanted to land up with Ruthie tuning into her Higher Self, I never got to that point. Because Bill's team played at 2 pm, so I had to stop in the middle of writing, so we could go to the swim pool and swim and be back in time for the game.

Which turned out OK, because I had never written so much in any of my chapters for the novel. I wrote so much that the next day I forced myself to write one sentence and then I gave up. I had exhausted myself. And so that next day which was Sunday, I got back into bed after the one sentence I had dragged out of myself, and dozed on and off and read Agatha Christie, and finally went to the machine, and I didn't even try to write at all.

I just went on my political forum and joined all the fun which was happening there. I said to myself "I am taking a day off," and I did have a great time on my political site. I hadn't been on for a whole week, and I posted and posted and posted and posted till I was worn out from posting. And then I read Agatha Christie till I went to sleep. I don't know if I even did emails, maybe some of them.

And then Monday I woke up to fresh start. I had thought I would continue from where I was interrupted, but I just wanted fresh start so much. And the day was so fresh too. I woke up to that cold misty air against my face, and that is all I wanted to talk about. And so I did.

I talked about the fresh misty air, and I talked about my project of buying bedding, so my bed would be toasty warm thru the ice cold winter nights.

And then yesterday morning I "knew" I had to go back and tell about what I had not gotten a chance to tell on Saturday before the big Wildcats football game.

And that was really odd in a way. Because you know I like to begin off with a gust of inspiration and the gust of inspiration comes from the sky and the wind and the birds and the sun and blue sky and the plants in my backyard and the trees. But I really knew it was the right story for me to be writing now. I am writing a novel, this is part of the story of the novel, a misty cold day and buying bedding is not. And I sort of liked the chapter, it never got hot and took off. It was amiable and low key. But telling about my friend tuning into her Higher Self, maybe that is the right note for that tale. And what does it matter anyway, it was such an odd story, such an odd chapter I guess you call it, because it had no beginning to it and it had no end.

I'm not saying the story itself did not begin at the beginning and end at the end. It was the writing of it, the experience of writing it. It was like picking something up, that is how it began. And then putting it down, that is how it ended. And nothing real seemed to happen between these two odd bookends. "I may as well stop here," I said at a certain point, pretty much the same way I had said "I may as well start here" when I began off.

"I may as well stop here" I said, and stopped and went out into the sunshine. And the whole thing (the experience of writing it) felt like gossamer, as if it had happened and not happened at the same time. And while I was lying in the lovely warm sunshine, and my Beanie was with me, I thought of something to add. And went back into the ice cold dark house and added. Then back into that heavenly sunshine, lied down in it, turned my face up to it and loved it. And thought of another thing to add. Went back into cold dark house with Beanie at my heels, added that, and then back into the lovely beautiful blissful sparkling sunshine.

And then Bill said "time to go to the pool!" and I said "perfect timing, I just finished!" and we got in truck to go to the pool. And I put all that conditioner in my hair to protect my hair from the chlorine and I had my bathing suit on under my dress. And when we got there, Bill said "pool is closed." It was Veterans Day.

So he said "I will go to two movies then."

And I said "I will edit that very long thing I wrote on Saturday, try to start fixing some of those typos."

And I said "Stop at Republican headquarters on the way home, it is right on the corner of Craycroft, so I can go in and find out what the elections are."

Apparently all the Districts are having election about the Republican committeemen for officers in that District. I had gotten something from the Republican Party but I assumed it was just more junk mail about the huge election on Tuesday, it arrived a few days before. And I had thrown it out with all the campaign mail which filled up my mailbox.

But I got email from my Ron Paul Tucson Group that "the whole reason we were asked to become Precinct Committeemen was so we could elect good officers in the Republican Party, those for liberty and peace." And the email I got said "you got notice from the Republican Party for when this election will take place for your District, and either you must run for Chairman, Secretary, or Treasurer in your District or vote for good people for those offices."

So I wanted to show up at that meeting where we elect officers in our District and I thought the Republican Party headquarters could give me the information, since I had thrown away their notice. But Bill parked in the parking lot and I tried to go in, and it was closed, so I guess it was closed for Veterans Day too.

But I now see it was the theme of that day. I was going to spend my afternoon taking care of all the things I had meant to take care of but hadn't gotten around to it. Now I was going to do it.

I had called Bill's sister the evening before, saying "we have to return Jim's computer day after Thanksgiving, and does she want to chip in to buy Bill a new computer," because it has been on my mind for 3 weeks-- how was I going to afford this new computer?

But Mary had not called back. Instead she had sent me email saying they are having money crunch themselves, and the repairman was not able to fix their washing machine, so they just went to Sears and bought a new one, because Sears offers a deal you can pay little by little each month, without any interest at all for 18 months, and that might be a good solution for me with Bill's computer.

I fiddled around with my email for a little while, but I really must have been in action mode. I just called Mary in San Diego. I said "it's fine that you can't chip in, I just want consultation on how to go about this, what are your suggestions of where and how?"

And Mary really encouraged me to check out the specials at Best Buy. She said "the super sales are all the day after Thanksgiving, at every store which sells computers, but I won't be able to find out till the Sunday before Thanksgiving what the sales will be, how much it will cost."

But she was very helpful to me. She explained they don't even make the old monitors anymore, I have to get a flat screen one. And we both realized that each time Compaq puts out a new computer, their older model goes on a good sale, and that happens all thru the year. And she was so definite and self-assured in all her answers to all my questions that it was a big help. And we got off the phone with her saying she would pray for me that I found the perfect computer at the perfect price.

So then I clicked on Best Buy to see what they were offering now. And sure enough they did have a Compaq computer for $349, which seemed like a great price to me. And they had a flat screen monitor for $150 which seemed like a great price to me.

So I called the one near Park Mall, which is near us, and after about a million phone rings, I got to talk to Angie, who was great. And we both said "this is a great price for a computer, and why wait till day after Thanksgiving, just come in and get it now." And she explained how the financing worked. I would get a bill in the mail from their bank, and I could pay $150 then and $50 each month till it was paid off. It would be like getting a credit card bill each month and I would not pay any interest. And that sounded perfect to me.

So I told Angie I would tell Bill when he got back from the movies and tomorrow after the pool we would come over and get it.

"I don't want to wait" I said.

"Good idea!" she said, "because then you will just talk yourself out of it."

And of course it did seem like it took a little courage.

So I called Mary back and she said "Great! Great! Great! Perfect, get it tomorrow!" And so I decided to do that. And I was so excited out of my mind, it seemed like such a big thing to be doing!

And then I did a bunch of little things, because there was still daylight to see. I got out the old comforters and put them in the new comforter covers I had bought the day before. And I remade my bed with the new covers I had bought. And put the old comforter in the new comforter cover for me. And brought the other old comforter in new cover to Bill's bed. And cut off some of the tags, and reorganized my bedding, so no matter how cold it got, I would be in a warm cozy nest.

And then when it started to get dark, the light was falling, I got under some of the covers to relax and think about things. And I thought "I really should call Jim and let him know about the computer sales I discovered in case he does want new computer, or flat screen, and to let him know we will return his computer and monitor right after we buy a new one." And mainly I was waiting for Bill to get home from the movies, so I could tell him "tomorrow we buy the new computer and monitor!"

And just when I was thinking about calling Jim the phone rang, so I thought "perfect! that is Jim calling me" and I raced into the other room. But it was Ruthie. And she said "so much is going on now with Soli my old boyfriend and Tom my new boyfriend, that I thought we could do Higher Self together on the phone now, if that is a good time."

I wasn't sure it was a good time because I was waiting momentarily for Bill to get home from the movies so I could tell him all about the new computer. While I had been lying down, I had thought of all the things Bill would say against the idea, and I had come up with ideas for it.

I knew the biggest thing against it was that Bill wasn't sure he wanted a computer. Yes, he wanted Jim's old computer, which Jim had said he would throw away. Bill said "if he is going to throw it away give it to him."

But that turned out to just be hot talk. When I asked Jim for it, it was clear he didn't want to just give it away. So Bill said "I will fix it for you and return it the day after Thanksgiving when all the big sales are." Which is how we had left it.

And Bill had set up that computer, and now had his own first computer and was happy with it. But he wasn't sure what he was going to do on it. Bill is hot for a computer if it is an old one someone is going to throw away, but very reluctant to spend $500 on a new one. This is why we have never bought him computer before. When push comes to shove and it involves money, he said "I don't want a computer." But each time Jim would say "I am throwing away this one," Bill would say "I want it."

But I knew Bill would want me to have back-up computer, he knows how much I love it and that I am on it all the time. And he would feel secure and happy that here was a new computer and monitor all set up, so Anne would not be without a computer. And this is exactly what happened when Bill did get home from the movies and I told him. At first he said "I don't know if I want a computer." But then he said "you have to have back-up one, if god forbid something happens to yours." So we decided we would do it.

But Bill was not yet back from the movies when Ruthie called, but I knew I would want to have this conversation with him when he did.

"Is this a good time to do Higher Self together?" Ruthie asked.

"It's fine" I said "but I have to get off when Bill gets home."

"Fine" she said.

And then I stayed on the phone while she prepared her chicken soup.

Apparently calling Soli in Cairo to cheer together about the election outcome, had opened the way for emails fast and furious between them. Plus Ruthie was baffled by the experience of the phone call. Other than that one time she had seen him when he was visiting old friends in NYC, and the one time she had called him when she was in Rome on the way to Muktananda's ashram in India, back in the early '80s, she really had had no immediate personal contact with him since they had been boyfriend and girlfriend all those years ago. All these years, the man in her mind, had been the man she knew all the way back then. And the relationship had been the one she had all the way back then.

She said "I had a wonderful conversation with his secretary, but the conversation with him was awful. He just went on and on, and I couldn't get in a word edgewise. And nothing he said interested me at all."

She said "I am falling out of love with my old boyfriend and falling in love with my new boyfriend." She said Tom had said "we have to sleep together all night, if we sleep together in same bed all night it will make us closer."

And so the night before, Ruthie had stayed all night. But she woke up in middle of night totally wide awake, and she was not allowed to move, because she said "we are both such sensitive sleepers we would wake each other up." And she couldn't get up and read a book, or do anything she would do at home if she woke up wide awake at 2 am, because it is such a tiny little cabin. So all she could do was lie there without moving and she was completely awake.

So she said to him "I am wide awake, I want to go home."

And he said "stay!"

And so she just lied there wide awake for a very long time, not falling in and out of sleep, having wide awake thoughts, and eventually she fell back asleep. They woke up in the morning, and the result was she felt so attached to him. And it scared her. And because she was scared, she thought about Soli. Thinking about Soli made her feel more detached about Tom, wondering what Soli thought about her and had he really loved her back then, what were his real feelings about her.

"You think being in love would be a wonderful thing" she said, "but I am hurting."

So we both tuned into our Higher Selves together so Ruthie could get information which would help her about both boyfriends, what was happening between her and Soli now and between her and Tom. And it is really very interesting what Ruthie's Higher Self explained to Ruthie, and which she said out loud to me on the phone as she heard it.

And this is what her Higher Self said. Basically what is going on, really doesn't have to do with the two men. The whole purpose of all of this, the reason both these men came into Ruthie's life now, is to give her kick in the pants, to push her on the road which leads to the great heart of love of the universe.

Ruthie's Higher Self explained to Ruthie, that her relationship with Tom, that she has to get past her big crush on him. "That it is not about her crush. It is to tempt her into wanting love, to tempt her into love, so she will arrive at that cocoon of total love and peace, which the great heart of love of the universe brings."

Her Higher Self explained "that neither man can give Ruthie all the love she wants, that no human being can offer that to another human being, that you simply can't demand it or expect it or insist on it. That it looks that way at first, when people first find love when there hasn't been any in their life, they become insatiable, and want more and more and more.

"But Ruthie has to be smart, she has to keep her balance. That what she does now, when she becomes anxious, her solution is to run around and distract herself. But instead she should relax herself. Breathe more! breathe deeply! take hot baths! everything which relaxes her. Try to meditate. And try to be still and go deeper. Because the only way she can reach that deep heart of the universe is by going deeper. And that is what she really wants and that is the purpose for all this."

Her Higher Self said "there are many ways a person could get a kick in the pants to go down the path which leads to the great heart of love in the universe. For instance they could lose their house. But Ruthie's kick to get her going are these two men coming into her life now."

Her Higher Self said "of course it is wonderful about Tom and it will get more and more wonderful and there will be more and more love. And same with Soli, they have a lot to share too."

Her Higher Self explained to Ruthie "that Soli had opened up her political heart, so now she is opening up his spiritual heart, because he has been way too cut off from all his feelings. And that the way to open his spiritual heart is not to talk about spirituality with him, but simply to love him. Not to criticize anything he does, just to accept him as he is. And that is the way he will open to being on the path to the great heart of love of the universe.

"All Ruthie has to do is love him, and the same with Tom. That it is a ripple effect. As Ruthie moves towards the great heart of love in the universe, it will ripple out to Tom and Soli, they will find they are on their way there too and from both these men it will ripple out to others. That Ruthie owes it to the world, and to these two men who she cares for so much, to do her assignment, to find her way to the great heart of love in the universe.

"And Anne's assignment right now, is, she has a lot of decisions to make, and she will consult with her Higher Self to make the wise decisions. And the result is Anne will start to have stability in her life, she won't be so nervous about everything all the time. Anne will start to have stability and confidence."

And then Bill walked in the door and said "I saw two movies!" Tuesday is dollar day, so he loves it he can see two movies for two dollars. And I wanted to tell him about the computer and also I didn't just want to ignore him when he walked in the door, and Ruthie's Higher Self said "Perfect! let Anne talk to Bill now." A lot of helpful things were said, it was a good session, and so Ruthie and I got off the phone without talking about what we had learned, or what her Higher Self said.

And Bill was hesitant about buying new computer next day. "Let me think about it" he said. And then came around and said "it is good idea," and turned on the football game. And he said "enough about it! let me watch the game!" And told me about the two movies he saw. And I went in to lie down and think about everything.

But as soon as I put my head on the pillow, I thought "why don't I check out Office Depot! They are on the way home from the pool and where I bought my 3 computers over the years and my monitors, maybe they have an old model Compaq on sale too."

I wasn't sure what time they closed, but I decided to give them a whirl. And I talked to Larry and he said their Compaq on sale is $250 and I went out of my mind with joy and said "I will buy it tomorrow." Their flat screen was smaller and cost $20 more but Larry said it is probably better than the one I found at Best Buy since he never heard of that brand, and his is Samsung, top brand!

So I told Bill all-excited, and said "I am going to call Mary," and he said "enough! just email her!" So I emailed her all excited and with joy.

And then it hit me about the rebates. Larry had mentioned that so casually. I realized it would mean I would not write out check for $260, I would have to write out a check for $110 more, and hope and pray those rebate refunds actually do arrive in the mail. They never did with the monitor. (But a year later I mentioned it at Office Depot, and they handed me the money.) Paying for both of them, without the rebate refund, makes it a whole lot more money. But they too have the deal where you can finance it without interest, so I thought I would do that, since it makes the money high enough to qualify, you have to spend $500 for it.

So then I called Larry back, and he said he has no time to sit on phone with me now, he is closing out the store. I said "how much more will I actually have to write the check out for tomorrow? how much is the rebates?" But he did not know. But he said he did find a bigger flat screen for the same price. "We have so many of them" he said, "in all sizes and with all features." He said he would be at the store tomorrow at 2 pm. So I thought we would come there after the pool.

And then I did something I never did before. Each time I bought my Compaq before, it was because my other computer had gone to heaven, so we stopped at Office Depot on way home from the pool, I asked "which is your cheapest computer?" and each time they had an old model Compaq at a good sale because the new model had come in, and I had just bought it.

But this time, yesterday evening, I went on my computer and looked at the one Best Buy had on sale for $340, and looked at the one Office Depot had on sale for $350, but gave two rebates for which brought it down to $250, and I discovered they were not exactly the same computer, one was a single something or other, one was double something or other.

And both sites had customer review about each computer, one review about each computer. The one at Office Depot described the pros and cons and it seemed to be fine. And the one at Best Buy said "this is the worst computer in the world, and I made a huge mistake to buy it, and Hewlett Packard" (I forgot that Hewlett Packard bought Compaq) "no longer has quality control over what they are putting out."

That was not an encouraging review, it made me not want to buy the one at Best Buy, I decided definitely to buy the one at Office Depot. And then I looked at flat screen monitors. And the Office Depot site said they have one for $150 and there were 8 reviews saying they bought it even tho they had never heard of this brand before, Acer, and they love it. And so I copied down the model number of it, because sure enough there are gazillion flat screens available, and I thought I would ask Larry if he has that one.

I had never researched computers or monitors before, I just walked into Office Depot and bought whichever was the cheapest and which the guy said was good.

My head was swimming, especially since in the customer reviews they talked about features which I didn't even know what they meant.

And then that was it. I clicked on my email, I had not read or answered any of my emails all day, but my head was swimming. I just wasn't in that place to communicate. And I clicked on *Letter from God* for that day and no way I was peaceful enough in my mind to read something like that.

So I just got into bed and tried to think about setting up Jim's email for him again when we return his computer to him, and it was a long night with a lot of wakefulness.

Which is why I woke up this morning and thought "a lot got accomplished yesterday" but I didn't think I wanted my days to be like this. But if Ruthie's Higher Self said my new life is going to be involved in a lot of decision making, and it will bring me stability and confidence, then haha maybe this is my new life.

November 14

Buying the new computer

Well new computer is bought, and flat screen monitor and printer with scanner. I don't envy Bill having to set that all up on big table in dining alcove, and then learning how to use it all. For someone whose only experience of computer is 2 weeks on that computer Sophia's son bought back in 2000, before computers were even towers, when the huge monitor sat on the box that the computer was.

Sophia's son was then living in Sedona. He had just finished law school at Berkeley, and when he and his wife had their baby daughter-- she wanted to go home to New York to be near her family-- so Sophia's son who had passed the Bar in California, then passed the Bar in Arizona, had to move to Brooklyn and study to pass the Bar there. Which I have no idea if he ever did, as he got hired for a company out there.

To leave Sedona for Brooklyn is not my ideal, as I have heard Sedona is one of the most beautiful places in the world. But of course I can understand. She had new baby, she wanted her family around, it is a new family member, and now there is a new baby boy too. Mark may not yet have passed the Bar in New York, but he has a precious little girl and a precious little boy. Altho Sophia said the company he works for doesn't pay him very much because he has not passed the Bar, they make him do all the work but do not give him the high pay.

In any case before they moved to Brooklyn, he brought the computer, the monitor, the printer, and gave it to Sophia, so she would have a computer, and said he will buy a new one in New York.

And Sophia never took it out of the box. Then Sophia's friend from Poland who loves Sophia, they are best friends, and who has a lot of money, said "Sophia, it is not good for you to be so isolated, you have to join the world."

And he bought Sophia fancy computer, a flat screen monitor when they first came out, and a printer, and set it up for her. And she called me up to teach her how to use a computer, and also how to do email. And I did go over there 3 or 4 times and I did the best I could. But Sophia never really made any progress because to learn computer and to learn email, you have do it. 3 lessons doesn't do anything. And she never uncovered her computer except when I came over for her lesson.

Altho when Sophia finished her screenplay, I think she hand-wrote it because she said she did all the writing at Barnes and Noble, and then Mark typed it all up for her. She tried to sell her screenplay and when she did not, someone told her "Turn it into a book! then when your book is best seller, the movies will buy it!"

The screenplay is her own personal experiences back in Poland during World War 2. As Sophia rightly said "they could not find that story anywhere else, only Sophia knows that story." So Sophia decided she would find someone to help her turn it into a book, altho she is just living on Social Security she does not have a lot to pay anyone.

But apparently heaven sent Sophia an angel. Some extraordinary wonderful young woman, I never met her, who came every day and sat with Sophia in front of her computer (as I had done) and Sophia told her what she wanted, and the girl turned it into a book.

And 2 months later when we met for our writers' meeting at Barnes and Noble, this was in June a few years ago, Sophia handed me the whole typed up book. And I sat there and read the first two chapters, and it was great.

When Sophia was 19 years old in Poland, she met on the train a young Jewish man at University the same age as Sophia. They became the closest of friends, and finally he confided in Sophia his experiences in a concentration camp when he was a little boy. It has been Sophia's raison d'etre to write that all down, and she was working on the screenplay the whole time I was at the Swim Club with her. The story of how she met him, their friendship, and what he told her. "I cried on every page" she said, "that my beloved friend went thru this." It is not a story I would want to read, I loved crying at books when I was 10 years old, *Black Beauty* and *Bambi*, but now I cannot take it. But Bill is very interested. He said "This is real history, and historians may not know about it, and Sophia should send her book to them, they will want to know this."

They stopped having the writers' meetings at Barnes and Noble once a month, so Sophia and I are now going our separate ways when it comes to writing. I no longer know what she is doing, and she doesn't know what I am doing. The last time I saw her, she was trying to sell her book, writing query letters to editors, and also planning out her second book. Apparently Sophia's grandmother in Poland, or some friend of the family or acquaintance, gave Sophia recipes for beauty creams, which had been handed down in her family forever.

And, altho back in Poland the nuns all wanted Sophia to be a chemist, she had genius for chemistry (I guess her high school was taught by nuns). And her father had a light opera company and Sophia had trained in opera. When an Ohio music teacher from a college was over there as an exchange student, this must have been way back, he fell in love with Sophia, married her, and brought her back to Ohio.

And what Sophia had actually worked at all these years in USA, was for Helena Rubenstein, giving facials in Tucson. She did it at the Helena Rubenstein spa in the big fancy hotel in the foothills here.

But Sophia, who has a scientific mind, at some point decided "I want to know what is underneath all this," and did a whole study of the skin. And she also studied law here on her own. Sophia is a brilliant woman. So in all her years of work and study in skin care, she does think she is the perfect person to write this book, about those 12 amazing recipes for skin care, those secret recipes brought down from the mountains there.

Sophia actually found a writers group to belong to, way downtown, near where she lives. And even tho she said "I will try to get you in, Anne" I have not heard from her. Which is fine with me. Sophia likes going to things, but I like just waking up, looking out my open window, and writing. My life suits me as Sophia's life suits her.

But in any case, as soon as her friend from Poland set up her new fancy expensive computer, monitor, and printer, she offered to sell Mark's old one for 200 dollars. And Jim at the pool bought it.

It sat in boxes in his garage until last year, actually about 8 months ago, when Jim got it out, set it up. Because his mom had gone to Heaven, and Jim had been taking care of her, and they were both living on her Social Security. He set up the computer so he could go on email to look for a job. At some point he decided the computer was broken. His friend gave him an old laptop. And when that stopped working, he said "A pox on both your houses!" and decided he would throw them all in the garbage. But Bill took Sophia's son's old Gateway computer, got it to work, and has been fooling around with that for past two weeks.

But he hasn't been on very much, he still calls me in when he wants to write an email, for help.

Which is why I don't envy him, having to learn this ultra modern computer, ultra modern screen and ultra modern printer with scanner. I am so relieved I am still on my old computer, my old monitor, my old printer, where everything is already familiar and known. But it is like hearing footsteps approaching, I know it is only a matter of time before I will be thrust out of this comfortable nest, and have some of that stuff too. At least a flat screen monitor, I have a hunch is in my future. And maybe laser printer. Bill's printer is inkjet, but I saw the prices of laser printers have come down, that may be in my future.

I got a huge crash course on what is available now, and how much it all costs, because the day before yesterday I looked it all up on my computer, everything which Office Depot and Best Buy are selling. And then yesterday we actually went to Office Depot to buy. Jim wants his old computer and monitor back now that Bill fixed it, and because Jim doesn't have dough to buy new stuff, and because he has zero desire for a computer, he only wants it to do email to find a job. Jim said the instant he finds a job, he will never go near a computer again, and all of it goes in the garbage.

I really don't know how to describe the experience of going to Office Depot yesterday to buy all this stuff, and it is one of those experiences you wouldn't wish on your worst enemy.

We arrived after the swim pool at exactly 2 o'clock, exactly the time Larry says he arrives at work, I had spoken to Larry the evening before. Bill and I were in good mood, because when we had shown up at swim pool the day before, it was closed for Veterans Day, so it seemed very luxurious to show up at swim pool and have long lovely luxurious swim.

And after our showers we arrived there exactly at the dot of 2. I asked a young man "where is Larry?"

And he said "I am Larry," and he took us over to the Compaq computer he had on sale. It was $360, but if you do the two rebates it comes to $250, which is a great price. But I had very bad experience doing the rebate there, with the monitor I bought there 5 years ago. The rebate never came. But on a lark, two years later, when I happened to be in Office Depot, I mentioned it to them, and they made it up to me. The result is I am now iffy in my mind about the rebate, I have the idea I could get the refund and I have the idea I could not.

When he showed us the flat screen monitors, I asked about the one I had found on their website the evening before.

He said "this is it! it is $180."

I said "the one on the website said $150."

He said "maybe that is just for people who order it on-line."

I said "no, because I read the customer reviews, and a woman said 'I happened to be in Office Depot with my husband the other night and I found it.'"

And he looked it up on his computer, and he said "Look! the only one there is $180."

But luckily I had copied down the order number last night, and when we were leaving for the pool, and were out the door, I said "wait!" and went back and got it. And so Larry punched in those numbers, and sure enough it turned up, flat screen monitor by Acer for $150.

And he read all about it, and he said "this is perfect for you!"

And he said "let me check if we have it in stock."

And he punched in some numbers, and said "we do!"

And he went to get it. And I thought "good! my research the previous night paid off." Hahaha it paid off in 30 dollars. Plus the morning before we left, I had found the two coupons Office Depot offered and printed them up, and that was in my purse too, the 2 coupons came to 30 dollars.

We had just planned to buy the computer and the monitor, but when Larry showed us a printer scanner for 65 dollars I couldn't control myself, "we'll take that too" I said. I thought Bill could find a way to post his artwork on the web.

Larry said "I have to warn you, it says $65, but you have to buy the cord for $25, and the two inkjets, and the paper, and that jacks up the price a lot."

In fact it made the printer twice as much, but it went thru one ear and out the other, because I was lost in the glory of a printer for $65 which featured all those things.

So then we went to buy it all and that is when all the trouble began. Property taxes which I just had paid, first half year property taxes, were doubled. I did not want to make an outlay for $650 now, I have car insurance and home insurance coming right up.

And Office Depot offered that thing, if you spend $500, you have 18 months to pay it at your convenience with no interest. That is made for me!

But it was incredible all the information they wanted to qualify. Todd was doing it for me. And finally he couldn't keep going back and forth from his computer to the desk where I was waiting.

He said "come with me, we'll do it together."

And it was torture. It was as much information as if I were opening up a bank account or credit card, maybe more. We had to put in my whole financial history, everything! And by the time Todd finally finished, it probably took 45 minutes, it said "sorry not accepted, I can try again in 30 days."

So I said "OK I will write out the check for the whole thing now and pray," which meant I would put it on my credit card from my credit union, I would just pay their interest. But to my shock when I tried to use my credit card, which I used for everything, it said "not accepted," and I have no idea why.

So I said "OK put it on my VISA card." I don't like doing that because it is 30 per cent interest.

Then I showed Todd my coupons, and he punched in all the numbers for them, for that $30, and it said "not good for technology!"

But Todd said to make it up to me, for all the time we spent trying to get the Office Depot card, he found a way around it, and he was able to take 30 dollars off for me. I was deeply grateful.

I said "OK now help me do the rebate, last time when I bought the computer the clerk helped me."

Todd said "the last thing I ever expected was to do the rebate for someone."

It turns out we were talking about different things. The clerk who helped me last time had only xeroxed for me what I had to send in. When I asked Todd to do the rebate for me, he thought it was the whole deal. I had forgotten about the whole deal, what I had had to do when I got home to do it and it is a huge deal.

Todd looked at my receipt and discovered I got 3 rebates, one for 50, one for 60, and one for 50. Altho it is all for the same computer, maybe they just make it hard for you. I had brought 3 envelopes with 3 stamps, altho I had no idea why I had brought so many, and I put 3 stamps on 3 envelopes, filled out my return addresses.

And before Bill carried it all out to the truck, Todd borrowed a knife from someone and cut off the barcode on everything I had bought, they wanted that. And then he went in the back where the xerox machines were to photocopy what they wanted and to fill out the rebate thing on the sales slip.

And it took a whole hour. I couldn't believe it. I stood at the cash register for 45 minutes when he said "wait here!" And then I went to the back to find him. I thought I had misunderstood. But he was still working on it.

And then finally he handed me the 3 envelopes, they all went to the same post box in Texas, but they were each addressed differently. And I guess he had to fill in the model numbers for everything and photocopies of sales slip. He was a saint to do that for me.

It was now 1 minute to 4 and the mail leaves post office at 4 pm each day, so we drove right to post office to put it in the box, and then Bill brought the stuff into the house.

And I ate and had a cigarette and collapsed on the bed.

And I was scared about spending all that money. I hadn't looked carefully at sales receipt, I just saw it came to $600 plus, and I had some idea I was spending $400 plus.

"Is this right?" I had asked Todd, but he showed me it was right.

I could not relax. And then I remembered how I had been turned down by Office Depot and I remembered how my credit card which I use all the time, had been declined, and I succeeded in totally scaring myself. And I couldn't see how it was a good thing I had just spent all this money.

I tried tuning into my Higher Self, who just kept assuring me "it is a good thing, I did everything right, I have nothing to worry about."

But it didn't help. Nothing helped me, and you know how that is, you get desperate and think nothing will.

I had tossed and turned about it for 2 hours. And then finally I began to compute everything in my mind. I hadn't actually looked at the sales slip. I remembered how much the computer was, how much the flat screen monitor was, and I had added those together in my mind. I knew how much the printer was and I made a stab at the power cord, $25 and ink jets and paper, $35, and a stab at tax, 10 per cent, and then I deducted the 20 dollars in coupons.

I remember now! I had just started to do this and was going to give up, I thought it would just take me to another anxiety place in my mind, and not help me.

But my Higher Self said "do it! keep going!"

So I had gone all the way. Deducted the coupons, deducted the rebates. I don't remember the figure I finally came up with, but suddenly I saw I had gotten an incredible bargain for everything I had gotten. And for some reason this relaxed me.

There was just no way, as anxious scared frazzled disturbed upset as I was, that I could not recognize this is an incredible bargain for what I had gotten. In fact it could be called a miracle. It was like a light piercing thru the darkness of my mind. I saw with my own two eyes I had gotten a great bargain, it was a great gift. It couldn't be seen any other way.

And I was able to recognize that was a good thing, that something good had happened. It settled me down. I stopped going over everything in my mind, I stopped being agitated.

I was left with only one concern, how come my bank credit card wouldn't let me use it? "Have I spent too much money" I wondered "and reached max?"

But I had suffered in my mind too much already, and had finally found peace about it, I just didn't want to get all worked up now, about what was going on with my bank credit card. I thought "I will be at the bank the next day to pay my credit card bill, I will find out everything then, and who knows maybe it is just a mistake."

The fact is it had been an amazing experience being in Office Depot with Larry. I had assumed a digital camera cost $1000 but Larry showed us they are now $130.

It means Bill could take his paintings in back yard and sunshine, take a pic of them and it would go right on his computer.

I said "this would be a good thing to buy in the Spring."

And Larry said "by that time, they will have them for less money and with more features."

He said "everything is like that now, if you wait, it is less money and more features."

And I guess that was the high point of being at Office Depot, the high point in the afternoon. It's not exactly Heaven or Santa Claus but a lot like both of those, that everything we could possibly want, or dream of, just gets better and better and costs less and less.

As if the universe is conspiring to make us happy, and give us gifts galore.

November 14

Beanie buries his cookie

It is a very pretty morning and I am up early and so are all the sparrows. O Beanie arrived with cookie in his mouth. It is so funny watching him with that big dog biscuit in his mouth. He is going out to bury it in a secret place in the yard. And he is acting like Black Bart. As if he is a pirate slipped off unobserved to secretly bury a cache of gold. Beanie arrived so silently in his yard, the only witnesses were the sparrows who flew off the piece of stale rye bread at his entrance. Then Beanie looked around surreptitiously and walked out of view.

He is so funny about those cookies. In the evening he is outside, taking in the night air, he likes it cold, he likes being in his cold yard under the moon and stars, he is a little wolf. Bill will be watching the game in his room, I will be in my room reading on the bed. And if Bill comes in to go to the bathroom, he will always poke his head into my room to see if Beanie is there.

"Where is Beanie?" he says.

"I don't know, he must be outside."

And then the funniest thing happens. Beanie dashes in from outside, he must have realized Bill was just outside my room, he makes mad dash, and I always think it is because he wants to rush in and say hi to Bill.

But it is because he had left his dog biscuit unattended on rug in front of my bed. He makes that mad dash when Bill is at doorway, past Bill's legs and right for the cookie and puts it in his mouth. And moves it. He has realized he has left a dog cookie unattended in my room and is convinced if he doesn't arrive fast enough and get it away, Bill will steal his cookie.

Bill and I watch in amazement. Beanie is so serious about it, so dead serious, and it is so illogical. Bill is the one who drives to Petsmart to buy Beanie his big box of dog biscuits and then brings it from the truck into the house. I put them in his big bowl so he can help himself to one whenever he wants. That Beanie lives in constant fear and has to be always on guard, that Bill will steal his dog cookie and eat it, is insane.

Beanie actually thinks the only reason Bill pokes his head into our room before he goes in to brush his teeth before going to bed, is to see if there is an opportunity to steal Beanie's dog cookie. Beanie races in from the far reaches of the yard and snatches it up just in time.

He is always so relieved and pleased he got there in time. He has to rush right past Bill's legs, and he removes it to safer place. I guess he is out there now with it in his mouth looking for a good place to bury it, that will ensure Bill never gets his mouth on it.

Beanie is always vigilant and spares no effort to keep his cookies away from Bill.

It's nice being up early again. Ever since the cold came in I would not get out of bed. I would lie there till I dozed off again, and wake up when it was sunny and toasty warm.

But I'm glad I got out of bed this morning. The early morning prettiness is the prettiest. And it is a beautiful day. And the fresh cold air is just delicious, if you are wearing two tops and two skirts. It is not freezing and hurting cold, just alive and happy.

November 15

A big wind

There is a wind, a real wind. It is blowing the trees about. It is blowing in on me now, on my face. It isn't a big wind and it isn't a little one, it is a medium wind, and sometimes it blows harder and sometimes it doesn't blow too much, but it is always blowing. Everything out there is in motion because the wind is blowing the tree branches and the leaves are still on the trees. It is like a dance, when the orchestra speeds up its tempo the dancers dance faster, when orchestra slows down dancers nearly stop. Except my trees are dancing to the wind.

I had peculiar dreams all night long. Hahaha I wonder if that is what a novel is, fiction is. The dreams had a plot and story line and mystery and suspense and bad guys in it.

The dreams took a few things from my life now and wove this whole mystery suspense plot out of thin air.

Because Soli had asked Ruthie on the phone if she had heard anything about Francis Cohen. And Ruthie had asked me. And Francis had been my best friend from babyhood till I was 12 years old. I said to Ruthie "I know her, we used to play dress-up together when we were little girls."

And Ruthie said "write me what you know about her and I will send it to Soli on email."

And so I wrote Ruthie about my friendship with Francis when we were the age of nursery school. And then I said "because Francis went to communist camp every summer, and loved it so much, she convinced me during a sleep-over to go also. And the summer I was 12 I went for one month. And that is when the friendship ended. But I fell in love with camp, and after that I spent my summers in camp instead of with my family in the Adirondacks." And I told Ruthie in the email a little about what that camp was like, so she could send it to Soli.

Meanwhile Soli was telling Ruthie a lot about Ted Axelrod, who was his best friend in college. And that name was so familiar to me but I didn't know how. And I think last night I wondered if he had been at that camp as a counselor or training counselor.

I must have been thinking about that camp before I went to sleep, because all my suspense drama mystery dreams revolved around it. Except they were all on the internet. My first dreams, when I got into bed, were about posting on the internet. I kept rewriting my posts in my mind, trying to say exactly what I wanted to say.

And in the last of the dreams, it was as if everyone who had been to that camp, Higley Hill, we were all on a website together, talking to each other.

And somebody had found that website and found me, and was on it too, there were two of them, but the main one was always giving me bad advice. That was the drama of the dream, how to deal with that person who was always trying to steer me in the wrong direction.

Like all big dreams there were thousands of little details in it too, but that was the conflict part of the dream, the problem I was trying to solve in my dream. I wondered if I should come out in the open and say "stop it!" Or just ignore the bad advice and pretend it wasn't happening.

And then I woke up to this wonderful wind and this beautiful day.

This is a developing time because a huge change happens tomorrow in the life of the Tucson swimmers. All the pools close for the winter except one. We are all going to be pushed out of our habits. Today is the last day Fort Lowell pool will be open. We all called out to each other "see you tomorrow," and even tho none of us usually swim on the same days, very few are there every day, because today is the last day, everyone will come today, to take advantage of the last day of it,

And none of us knows what will happen starting tomorrow when all the lap swimmers from all the pools converge on Jerry's pool at Catalina High School, the one open pool. It is like the last day of grade school before summer vacation, knowing none of us would be back in this pool for 4 months, and knowing we wouldn't see each other for 4 months. We certainly won't see any of the lifeguards, they have been let go for the 4 months. And we don't know which of our fellow lap swimmers we will see at Jerry's pool.

Before I went to sleep I thought about change. I thought how even tho this would not be called a good change, that all change is exciting and interesting and brings in the new.

And it causes changes before it happens too. Our entire relationships with each other at Fort Lowell pool have totally changed in anticipation of the pool closing. We have a topic of common interest to talk about, something which affects all of us. And we are all in the same boat, we don't know what will happen.

And we have all become very chatty with each other; and Fort Lowell pool and its swimmers are not usually chatty at all. There is that feeling that we won't see each other for 4 months, so things have gotten much more personal.

For the first time in shower room yesterday Kathleen asked me about Bill's painting and about my writing, and she told me all about making pots as a potter. We had long conversation and I guess you could say our first real conversation in all the years we have been swimming together. All the rest was chit-chat under the shower. We never stood in the changing room for long time and talked seriously before. We never acted like we were real friends and not just pool friends.

I think it is because it is like being in a class in 6th grade and next year we will all be in junior high school and in different classes and just be brushing past each other in the hall. That is the feeling of it.

And the day before Tucson public television came to interview Russ at the pool. I don't understand it. When I arrived, the lifeguard said "the television cameras just left, you missed them." And he said "they interviewed Russ."

I can't make heads or tails of this. If Tucson public TV came to do a special about the pools closing and came to our pool, why wasn't Samantha, the head lifeguard, in the shoot? And why did they only interview Russ, who doesn't swim, who walks back and forth in the lane for 45 minutes as his exercise program. But of course we are all going to tune in to watch Russ be interviewed at our swim pool on the Monday before Thanksgiving on "Arizona Illustrated." It is a huge deal for us all to watch this. And they told Russ when it would be on and he told the rest of us. We can't wait to watch Russ on TV.

So you can see from my point of view change has brought a lot of new things into my life...

November 16

We move to Tucson

It is a time of great beauty on the desert. And this is when I moved here. No wonder I woke up the first morning and looked out and it took my breath away. I could not believe I had moved to such a beautiful place. We had arrived in the middle of the night so I had no idea what it looked like. I discovered it the first morning and it looked like this.

I am up much earlier than I have been waking up since the cold began. So it is an earlier morning beauty. It is pretty. There are so many more shadows, I guess the sun is not very high yet. So it looks like cool dense banks of green in some places out my west window, in side yard before Caren's shed. I am not used to the sight of dense vegetation. Out my regular window into big backyard is trees scattered. I am seeing now where all the bushes are growing into each other, I had no idea vegetation had grown that dense in that side yard. Of course it's beautiful, there is nothing like luxurious vegetation.

And somehow because it is still in cool shadow, the sun is not shining on it, it looks so much thicker. Birds are flying into it and out of it and alighting on it too. They must have nests in there, or they just like it.

We arrived in Tucson November 17th, 17 years ago. We had one-way tickets. When my Uncle Gus came from Rochester to Berkeley where my mom now lives, I wasn't clear from my brother's emails if he had actually moved or was looking around. "He had a one-way ticket" my brother said, and I knew that he moved.

My mother had a one-way ticket too when she left Electchester in Flushing and came to Berkeley 9 years ago. 4 years later her brother bought a one-way ticket from Rochester and joined her there.

And 7 months after she moved, Ruthie bought one-way tickets for her and her son Davy and moved to San Diego.

Only Gene bought a round-trip ticket. His return ticket to New York is still somewhere in his stuff. He moved here 5 years ago. I guess buying a one-way ticket means the decision is made, you aren't coming back, but buying round-trip ticket, having return ticket with your stuff, means you have decided to put off deciding.

My uncle Gus moved to Berkeley when he was in his nineties. My brother said he arrived with golf clubs and two suitcases and that was it. He left everything behind in Rochester where he had lived his whole life. The instant his house was sold, he bought his one-way ticket.

My mom arrived on her one-way ticket a year before her 80th birthday. She wanted some of her stuff, so a moving van moved some out. It wasn't very much stuff, the moving van filled up at a lot of other houses before it drove across country. My mother is not into stuff but the few things she wanted, she wanted.

I don't think Ruthie took anything, she was fleeing from her husband then. I did not know anything, all I knew was she was in San Diego, and since it was summer I thought it was summer vacation. And then it seemed she didn't go back, and I found out she had moved there.

Bill packed up my computer and printer and monitor, and a few other tiny items and sent them by UPS to my aunt, so they would be waiting for us. And packed up the rest of what we wanted, to just send by the post office. Most of it was all my old writing, there were boxes and boxes and boxes of that. And a box with his climbing gear and box with our clothes, we didn't take too many clothes, and a box with books, we didn't take too many books.

The boxes of all my old writing is still in its boxes, in the closet now to my left. I forgot I used to write on blue paper. Boxes and boxes of typewriting on blue paper. The stories which were typed up and edited are in my file cabinet, there are not so many of these, but there are a lot, maybe 50, maybe 100, I don't know.

I've often wondered if I will ever look at and read those boxes and boxes of old writing, on that blue paper, and so much of it with faded typewriter ribbon. I wrote it all on that portable electric typewriter that we all liked so much back then. I would keep using the same ribbon till you could practically not see the words. And sometimes the paper itself was old and torn.

It seems crazy to have done that now, but maybe artists are just peculiar. I see Bill do the same thing. He has all kinds of new high quality art supplies in his closet, but instead of painting on canvas he will paint on old newspaper. It makes it harder later on, if it turns into something he likes. But I understand why it was easier to start it on old newspaper, rather than getting out fresh canvas.

At the time you say you are doing it to save money, and then later you yell at yourself for being cheap. But now I think starting is hard, and sometimes it is just easier if it feels like no big deal.

He gets out old newspaper, I would put the old blue paper in the machine and begin typing with the old faded ribbon. It's a soft way to begin, without everything being new and hard and spanking new. You trick yourself into starting by not making a big deal about it.

Writers no longer have slush piles, we do everything on the computer. But they were called slush piles back then. You would write every day and the pile would grow bigger and bigger. And then you'd put it in a huge folder in your file drawer and begin another slush pile.

But you'd remember the stories which made an impression on you, just a few for each huge slush pile, and get those out and type them up and edit them, and type it on good paper. And those would be your real stories. And then you would forget everything in your slush pile.

Altho all those slush piles are now in the closet to my left. I have not even opened the door to that closet in a few years. And I have not gone near those slush piles in boxes since we moved here.

A whole life in New York City is in those slush piles. It's funny that that is all in my closet now, to my right, and all in some closet in my mind too. And who knows if I ever will take any of it out, from either closet, the one in my mind or the one in my room. Probably not.

(from my blog)

Leaving New York

I didn't tell anyone we were leaving except our two families, my father provided the funding for it. And I wrote to Bill's parents in San Diego to tell them. Altho I did tell my friend Irene, we were on the phone all day together back then, we were best friends and we talked about my move a lot.

But I didn't tell my neighbors, or all my friends and acquaintances in the neighborhood, because I was in shock about the move. I thought it would help me if each day was normal, until we actually did it. I didn't want it to be the topic of discussion with everyone. I wanted to be treated as if I were still living in New York and always would, so things would not change.

I told one person, Joey. He was the big brother of a guy I knew in the '60s, Victor. And I used to see Joey a lot while I was walking the dog, we had become friends.

I said "I am moving to Tucson," this was in the school playground where I was throwing the ball for my dog.

"So what else is new!" he said.

He didn't believe me for an instant. Back in New York everyone says they are going to move, but no one ever does move. It was very interesting being faced with complete and total disbelief. I thought there is no way to convince someone who doesn't believe you for an instant; what can you say, "I am really going to do it!" they would just laugh. So we had parallel conversation until I happened to mention "the address of my new Tucson apartment is on East 2nd Street."

And all of a sudden he said, "You rented an apartment there! Then you must really be going to move! Wait this is big, let me buy us both a container of coffee, I want to treat you." And I was gratified that now Joey believed me.

He came back with coffee for both of us, and he said "I know all about Tucson."

"Tell me about it! What is it like?" I asked.

He said "it is middle class and you will have to dye your hair."

And I tried to picture dying my hair red. Everyone dyes their hair red when they dye their hair for the first time. We must all secretly long to be redheads.

The old lady, Mary, had all her stuff set up on the sidewalk in front of my building to sell, and some guys were helping her. And I told them I am moving to Tucson and one of the guys said he had been there.

"What is it like?" I asked.

"There are not many trees" he said.

Which is all I knew about Tucson before I arrived. That I would have to dye my hair and there were not a lot of trees. Altho my Tucson aunt, in one of her conversations, had mentioned something about "on the desert," so I realized I was moving to the desert. So I pictured Tucson as Arabia as I had seen it in movies. Which is why I was so taken aback and floored and delighted, when I arrived and found all the flowers here.

My friend Helene, I had told her, she still lived in my neighborhood then, offered to give me the phone number of her friend who has a car service, to drive us all to the airport. And so I called him and the arrangements were made.

And you can imagine my surprise, the Sunday morning before we left (we left in the afternoon of that Sunday) -- when I had my dog Clio at the handball courts and was throwing the ball for her, the young man who was sitting there, who looked a little wasted, as if he had been up all night-- every morning when I threw the ball for Clio at the handball courts, he came in with a container of coffee and looked wasted and talked with me --

I said to him "I am moving to Tucson."

And he said "I know! I am going to drive you to the airport." I was so surprised! But I liked it that someone who knew me and who knew Clio was going to be our driver.

I didn't tell my neighbors till the morning I left, that Sunday morning I told each one. Altho I must have told Carmine the day before, because when he told his friends in the saloon, he couldn't remember where it was I was moving. So he said "here! write it down for me," so I wrote down Tucson Arizona, so he could show it to them.

I didn't tell my neighbors because I was so close to them and had so many emotions about leaving them. And I didn't tell the people I was closest to in the neighborhood for the same reason.

And when we sat on the floor in the Newark airport for 5 hours, waiting for our plane, at some point I did start to cry. That is when it hit me for the first time. Before that I had just been thrilled that we had actually succeeded in escaping New York. I had wanted it for so long, and it had seemed impossible, and now I was doing it.

But in the Newark airport it hit me what I was leaving.

"I am leaving behind all this love" I thought, and began to wipe away tears.

But my Higher Self said "I would never take you away from love, Annie, you will have even more love in Tucson." And that reassured me, comforted me, and calmed me down.

A red sun was just setting in Newark when we boarded the airplane. Clio was in a dog carrying case in the baggage department and of course my heart was with her. I had made sure we took a flight which did not involve changing planes because I did not want Clio lost in the changing of planes. Altho we made two stops, where passengers deboarded and enboarded. We flew thru the night all across America. Altho I still remember seeing all the lights of Phoenix when we stopped at Phoenix.

We were such inexperienced travelers, but luckily my aunt had arranged for the guy who picks her up in his limo, to wait for us in the Tucson airport and drive us to our apartment. It was comforting to us he had one earring and looked like a punk rocker from the East Village. And he helped us find the baggage department so we could collect Clio. Then we got in his limo and drove thru the dark to our new apartment.

After living in our tiny tenement for so long, we were breath-taken by the beauty of the apartment. I could not believe my luck.

"I wonder how long we will be here?" Bill said, as we saw what a great apartment it was.

I was dumbfounded by the question. "We will be here forever" I said.

I had lived in apartments my whole life. I assumed if you find a beautiful apartment at a bargain rent, of course you stay here forever. It is a dream come true..

But exactly one year later we moved into our house. I hadn't realized Tucson was a place where you could expand.

11/17/08

I slept late

I slept late. I was up at 5 am, it was still dark. I put up the coffee, I turned on my computer, I made buttered toast, and took the cup of hot coffee and buttered toast to bedroom. I also changed my top to thin gray jersey with sparkles on it, it seems a warming spell is coming in. I saw the beautiful moon and beautiful stars as I walked out one back door and in another.

When I had gotten up at midnight, I had seen my doggie lying on cold earth in middle of yard under moon and stars, he likes that. But when I woke up at 5, he was on top of my feather bed with me, and did not stir when I put on the coffee. He likes sleeping out under the moon and stars, but finishing his night's sleep on top of feather bed with me.

I dreamed about Bill's kitty, in my dream she was

palling around with another cat, a grey striped one. She is tiger lily colored, she is a beauty. I must have drank my hot coffee and ate my buttered toast and put my head back on pillow. Because next thing I knew I heard Bill call out "Good morning Anne." And I see the morning is well advanced. Beanie waited for me to get up.

And now I am in here looking out at another very very very pretty day. I can even see some of the mountains to the west and they are purple colored. And the sky is a pretty blue. It is cloudless of course, this is the season of our beautiful weather.

Yesterday was an odd day. The wind had blown for two days and two nights, it was still blowing yesterday. And for some reason I knew it meant something. It had to mean something new was being born, something new was coming in. And when I stopped reading my mystery on bed to get in truck to go to swim pool, I was surprised how absolutely nervous I was the whole trip there. I could barely contain my nervousness. I thought it was connected to yesterday was first day of new swim regime, we would all converge on Jerry's pool and I would see what it was like.

It was crowded but I got a lane. And the water was

cold, as it always is at Jerry's pool. If only he would warm it up like the other pools. And I had my swim and the swim was fine, but I was still a little in a state.

And then I did my shopping at Sunflower Market, I wasn't as nervous, but I found it hard to shop instead of easy to shop. And my mind wanted to make such a big deal about every little thing. I noticed that thru-out the day, any little thing which went wrong threw me for entire loop.

They had London broil on spectacular sale, so I put that up at slow boil for Beanie, altho I knew Bill would have some with his dinner too. And then I read some more of my mystery. And I must have come in and thought I would fix the typos on what I wrote yesterday. And that is when I discovered the nervousness had broken out of all proportion. I could not fix one typo for the life of me. And after that I knew all I wanted was to get this nervousness to go away, it was starting to scare me. I was becoming nervous about being nervous. I was losing confidence that things would be normal again.

And also, as I put on some lights, it must have been around dusk, I had the odd thought which I had been having over past two days, that I was being pushed down a birth canal, as if I were being born. And so I read my mystery some more, and even dozed for an instant, and I noticed the doze totally relaxed me and I felt better.

And then I thought "I am marching right back to my machine, I don't want to think I am so nervous I have conniptions when I look at the screen, I am going to do my email and post on the internet, and I am going to bring everything back to normal."

And I answered my email and that made me feel a lot better, things seemed regular again. And I read a channeling. I wanted to read it because the title was "What is going on right now, you have graduated." And I thought maybe it would explain what was going on with me.

It was one of those ones which is hard to read, but for some reason I was able to read it right off the page. And the one thing which struck me in it, is she said a multi-dimensional shift has happened.

Then I found Arlene's email from her mom, she had forwarded it to me, saying "Mother has arrived in India." Arlene's mom still lives in Detroit, but she spends every ice cold winter with Arlene's sister who lives in India. And her mom described her flight. There was lay-over in Chicago, the weather was so bad, the airlines put them up in fancy hotel for the night and served them 5 course meal in fancy restaurant. Arlene's mom had great flight, they put her in first class and served champagne as soon as she got back on plane. And she described arriving in India. O yes she had loved the movie "The Kite Runner" they had shown. Then she arrived in India and now she was looking forward to all the interesting conferences she planned to attend there.

I forwarded the email to my mom. Arlene's mom is 3 years older than my mom and I thought it would interest her the adventures a woman her age was having right now.

Ruthie and I and Arlene all met in women's liberation back in 1968. Back then women's liberation (when it started) was wild hippy chicks, and Ruthie and I and Arlene were wild. A tiger does not change its spots, and even tho we have all settled down into being groovy housewives now (which I now realize was our destiny back then) there is a revolution in consciousness on our planet now, and we are part of that.

I had forgotten all about Alfredo Leonardi till Sophia was looking for film director to send her screenplay to, and I realized I know an Italian film director. I met him when Ruthie and I were school teachers at PS 110 on Delancy Street.

(from my blog)

Ruthie and me and Alfredo Leonardi

When I was teaching Sophia email and internet, I said "let's look up the guy I was friends with before I met Bill, he was Italian from Rome who was a film director, if we can find his email on google I can write an email to him asking if he will read your screenplay."

Sophia was totally into this and so was I. So I wrote down his name on her pad for her to type in, Alfredo Leonardi, and we googled it. There seemed to be a lot of movies directed by Alfredo Leonardi and starring Marco Leonardi, who I figured was the little boy, his son, when his wife came at the end of his visit to NYC and they went back to Rome together. Finally one of the entries was for a film collective in SoHo in Manhattan which lists Alfred Leonardo movies to buy and the film collective had an email. So I said "OK finally an email address, I will write to them and ask them to forward it to Alfredo Leonardo."

"Great" Sophia said.

So she got up and I sat down in her computer chair. And I composed my email outloud as I was writing it. At the top I wrote "will you kindly forward this email to Alfredo Leonardi since we were old friends."

Then I wrote, "Dear Alfredo, do you remember me" and I wrote my maiden name. And I said how I had stayed in the same apartment in the East Village in Manhattan where he had visited me for very long time till I moved to Tucson Arizona. That I met my husband a year after he returned to Rome. That I remembered the nice times we had, going to the beach together, and when I jumped out of the canoe.

I said how my friend Sophia wrote a screenplay and is he willing to read it. Would he send it to another director if it is not for him. And I gave my own email address cause I said I am on Sophia's computer. And would he write back and say hi to me because it would be fun for us to say hi again. And I sent my love to his wife and son.

Both Sophia and I were delighted with my email. I changed the font to make it prettier and then I did spell-check which picked up one mistake. I had said "I am no longer wild but I am not conventional." And I had put two "i's" in wild. So spell-check corrected that. I showed Sophia how spell-check takes out the misspelled word and replaces it with the rightly spelled word, she was impressed. We were both satisfied with my letter.

"I hope the gallery sends it to him" Sophia said.

"I hope so too" I said.

Of course it was tremendous fun for me to be writing to my old friend Alfredo Leonardi. We had been best friends, I have total warmth for him, and I never would have emailed him except for Sophia wanting someone in the film industry to read her screenplay.

I am curious if Alfredo will write back. I have never kept track of the boys who walked in and out of my life before I met Bill. At the time of course I was involved with the boys I had crushes on, and the boys who were just my best friends I didn't think so much about. But now I don't remember so well the boys I had crushes on and I remember perfectly the ones who were just my best friends, because those are the ones I shared my life with.

Alfredo and I hit it off right from the start because we were so relaxed with each other. He wasn't at all what I expected when Anna from Rome, who I had met the week before in the laundromat and who invited me to a party at her apartment that evening, said she had given my phone number to her friend Alfredo, who was film director from Rome.

This was the time of Marcello Mastroianni, Michelangelo Antonioni, etc. I thought I was being fixed up on a blind date with Marcello Mastroianni.

I guess he must have met me at school where I taught and then we walked over to a luncheonette nearby for our date. And he was not one bit like an Italian movie star. He was very diminutive to start off, and he strikes me now as looking English somehow with his rolled-up black umbrella as he waited for me. I guess he wore dapper clothes too.

But since he didn't look like a movie star and I was not attracted to him I relaxed instantly. And for some odd reason that I can't explain we totally hit it off in the luncheonette on Grand Street. It was an orthodox Jewish neighborhood, the neighborhood was like my Jewish neighborhood back in Queens except they were all orthodox. I guess it was a good setting for me to relax in.

And all I can say is from that moment till he left for Rome, or to be more exact when his wife and little boy arrived at the end of his NYC sojourn, Alfredo and I were inseparable.

What I did was take Alfredo with me to everything I did in my life, except go to work. He couldn't come to women's liberation meetings with me because those were all women, but I took him to everything else, and I guess we had our meals together in the restaurant on Avenue A too.

When I went to the beach on Long Island on weekends with Ruthie and Arlene I took Alfredo. His bathing suit totally embarrassed me. He wore a teeny-weenie white bikini men's bathing suit. I didn't say a word but Alfredo looked around Jones Beach and said "I see I am the only one wearing a bathing suit like this."

"Yes!" I said pointedly.

When Arlene called up me and Ruthie to invite us to the week-end conference for socialist Jews at a bungalow colony in the Catskills, I invited Alfredo. I have no idea what Arlene's group was all about. We went to the meetings and there were big fights. But I had only wanted to spend a weekend in the country. That is when Ruthie and me and Alfredo paddled in the canoe and smoked pot and I got stoned, took off my clothes, and swam naked to shore.

I alluded to this in the email I wrote him from Sophia's computer yesterday, since he had told me next morning it had made a big impression on him. I thought what made a big impression on him was my adventurous act of jumping out of canoe and swimming to shore. But when he detailed the big impression, it wasn't about what I had done, it was about me naked. Because we were just best friends and not boyfriend and girlfriend, I had not let him finish telling me how much he had enjoyed that.

But when I was writing a "remember-me" email all those years later, I figured that would reawaken his memory if he forgot me.

The last time I saw Alfredo was at Lynn's women's liberation party. His wife and little son were there, and his wife was blond and pretty and wore wrap-around skirt and was very interested in women's liberation. She was a very nice girl. Alfredo and I really were two ships which pass in the night. It was easy come, easy go. He waltzed into my life so easily, he waltzed out of it so easily. It never occurred to me to try to hold on to the friendship.

In fact I never gave him a thought after he left till I was writing a story about my days with Ruthie in women's liberation, and I remembered how Alfredo, me, and Ruthie had gone to that conference at the bungalow colony, and that brought back my time with Alfredo to my mind.

And I remembered him again when Sophia said she is looking for someone in the film industry. And I thought I know an Italian film director....

November 18

Sherry goes to Disneyland

Well another beautiful morning in paradise. I can understand now, when I moved here this same week 17 years ago, and pulled back the curtains the first day and saw what an absolutely beautiful day; and then pulled back the curtains the next morning and saw what an absolutely beautiful day; and how that happened every morning for whole first week, I thought "this is how it is here, this is what I moved to, this incredibly beautiful paradise."

I did not know I had arrived at the advent of this astounding prettiness. Now I understand why, when I went into a plant store to buy a begonia, the woman in the plant store said "it is so beautiful today, I wish I were out there instead of in my store." I thought it was always like this, I didn't know why she said "today is such a beautiful day," and why my aunt Celia exclaimed on the beauty of the day too.

After a whole week of it, Bill and I wondered to each other if we wanted every day to be the same, we were used to each day being wholly different weather back in New York. ("What if I get sick of beautiful days" Bill said, reading my mind.) But now I can't think why I thought I could ever get tired of endlessly beautiful days. It just seems natural and right and wonderful to me, and gift from the universe. Altho now I know December brings our winter rains, it is not always like this. But O it sure is nice.

Well there was a lot of suspense driving to Jerry's pool on the first Monday, yesterday, of the new swim regime. I had gotten a lane on Sunday the day before, the first day of it, but Sunday is an atypical day. Monday everyone would have returned to their routines. It was more crowded than usual but Bill and I each got our own lane, perfect!

When I walked in the first thing I said to Jerry was "If only one pool is open now, can't you heat it two more degrees, 81 is just not warm enough in winter, just two degrees warmer would make all the difference, then I could relax in the water."

Jerry gave me the same song and dance he always gives me every winter, when he "proves" to me 81 is really warm. I wasn't going to let him get away with it this time, I was going to hold my ground. But a woman just leaving the pool came up to me in the middle of it, and said "the pool is wonderful today, just wonderful."

So I said "OK, she says it is wonderful, I won't beg you till next month to heat it up two degrees."

Of course it was a little on the chilly side when I first got in, but then it did turn wonderful. And when I saw Jerry standing at the lifeguard stand talking to the lifeguard, I said "it's nice, it is really nice."

He said "maybe next time you will go in the water first, before you tell me how wrong it is, and yell at me."

It never crossed my mind that I had upset Jerry by imploring with him to make the pool warmer. I spent the rest of my swim bending over backwards to make it up to him. But each time I said "it is perfect, I love it, you did great, this is heaven," he said "next time you won't yell at me."

He said "I hope you will remember this when the bad days of winter come."

I had even thought of going over Jerry's head. When Bill and I were coming back from Fort Lowell pool on Saturday, the last day the other pools were open, and of course Fort Lowell really was heaven, Samantha keeps it toasty warm, Bill had said "if only Jerry would heat his pool another two degrees, now that all the others are closed."

Bill said "I won't ask him that, his feelings will just get hurt."

And I said "it doesn't do any good, he is so stubborn, he just insists it is warm."

And then we both said how stubborn Jerry is. And I said "well maybe I should talk to his boss, the Mayor, he has to do what the Mayor says."

And I actually planned out with Bill on the ride home, how he would drive me down there, he doesn't want to come in he wants to wait in the car, and I would go in and ask the Mayor to tell Jerry to warm up his pool and also to make the showers hot in winter. I really planned to do this, I thought it was a reasonable request, and I knew asking Jerry to do it would get me nowhere.

But I impulsively asked Jerry myself as soon as I entered yesterday. And the upshot of the whole thing is, Jerry won. If imploring him to raise it two degrees resulted in hurting his feelings, then I will not do or say anything else. Jerry can have it his way. Altho if it is a freezing cold day and his pool is freezing cold, I know I will say something. Jerry, who knows everything, must already know that. Because he said to me "I hope you will remember this when the really bad days of winter come." He knows I will open up my mouth. He knows me better than I know myself.

Last winter I had Kathy and we cornered him about it. But this winter Kathy is in Berkeley, her lesbian partner got accepted into divinity school there, and they are both living there till her girlfriend Angela finishes school. Kathy doesn't like cold water either. And last winter she joined a club for a few months because they keep the water at 85 degrees, I had found that club, it is very inexpensive, and I was going to join too to just have warmer water in winter. But when I arrived to join, they had put a bubble over it for winter, and I love to swim under blue sky and sunshine. But Kathy chose the bubble.

Of course I love Jerry with all my heart, who in Tucson does not. He is the warmest nicest sweetest friendliest most helpful guy in the world. Whenever we arrive at pool and Bill discovers he forgot his bathing suit at home, I say "Wait! let me ask Jerry."

I tell Jerry "Bill forgot his bathing suit," and he goes in the storeroom where the new bathing suits for lifeguards are stored, and gets out a brand new one in Bill's size, Speed-o, Bill's favorite! and says Bill can keep it.

What an angel!

Bill said in the truck going home "we didn't see anyone from our old pool there, there were just the people who always swim at Jerry's pool," and then we speculated where everyone from our pool would go.

I did see Sherry in the shower room. She said last week was her birthday, and so she treated herself to a week in Disneyland, and this day last week was the day she had to return to Tucson, and she didn't want to come back, she dug in her heels and refused to go, and had to be moved kicking and screaming back to Tucson. She loved every second of her trip to Disneyland.

It's such a satisfying report to hear when you are both naked under the shower together washing your hair. To hear your friend say "it was my birthday, I treated myself to Disneyland for a week, I had such a wonderful time, everything was great, that I did not want it to end, I did not want to come back home."

And then she said she was going home to do yard work. I said "you work far too hard, Sherry."

She said "that is why I went to Disneyland, for a whole week I played, I did not do any work at all, I just played."

Sherry cleans people's houses for a living during the days, and then is always working on her house, yardworking or painting it, whatever. I never knew someone to work so much and work so hard.

Maybe it is an omen of the new wonderful times which are to come, which are just around the corner now. When we see each other in the shower and are catching up with each other as we wash our hair, we will all be telling each other what a perfect week we had, how everything was so wonderful we didn't want it to end, and be lost in the glow of our happiness.

It is quite an amazing thing this planetary change scheduled for winter solstice 2011. As I understand it that is like the due date the doctor gives the expectant mom, and just as babies are born a little earlier or a little later, so this will arrive a little earlier or a little later.

Of course I am counting on it arriving a little earlier. I have decided in my own mind a little earlier means any time after June 6th 2010 I can begin to expect it. And because 6 weeks from now the year 2009 arrives, and 2010 is just the year after that, it finally does feel like it is getting close.

The book I have about it explained no one knows the moment and the day it will arrive, it will arrive like a thief in the night. Which didn't really hit me till yesterday when I was thinking about it, and thinking it was starting to get close.

I thought "what will happen after June 6, 2010, will I wake up every morning thinking 'today is the day it could happen,' will I go to sleep every night thinking it could take place during this night."

It seemed totally amazing to wake up each morning, look out and see a beautiful day, and think "today could be the day it happens," and spend a day in breathless expectancy.

It never occurred to me before how interesting and unusual the period of anticipation would be. To wake up each morning and think "today could be the most wonderful day in the world, today the most amazing thing could happen, today all dreams come true."

What will it be like? Will it give a fizz of excitement to each day? Will I start to have fizzy days? It seems to me now I spent my childhood in that kind of state. I wasn't aware that I greeted each day with "today is the day all my dreams will come true," I woke up in excited anticipation. But one day in my late 20s I woke up without it. I woke up feeling "today will be an ordinary day and nothing will happen." I guess I lost my sense of wonder and of the miraculous. The fizz went out of my life, lol like flat soda.

But this thing is huge, and any day after June 6th 2010 we can start to expect it.... and that will be a trip.....

November 20

Seeing my cousin Pete at the pool

I am up before the sun. It is light out but sun has not risen above mountains. There is no sparkling sunlight, it is still dun colored. Little birdies have not yet left their warm nests, I guess they are waiting for the warm sunlight to come. I think dawn may have been very recent, it has filled in with light but that is all. Nothing is stirring yet.

There is still the chilliness of dawn. I am sitting in two pullovers by my open window. I see one very brave bird has arrived. It is a big turtle dove, hopping along the ground. All the rest I still hear chirping in their nests. She is all alone in my yard, moving very fast along the ground, I guess she wants her breakfast.

O she flew off. And now two sparrows arrived together, they're climbing in my tree, hopping from branch to branch. They flew off.

I see the first of color. The sun must have risen higher to give color. The tops of some trees are now golden. It is an unusual gold tho, more like the color leaves turn in autumn, not a bright gold, but a warm mellow color. O yes the leaves are a little greener looking and not as dun colored. The sun is bringing color.

I saw my Tucson cousin Pete at Jerry's swim pool yesterday. It was earthshaking when I first recognized him there 3 years ago. In fact I didn't recognize him, I had just said to a man who was waiting for a lane "you can share with me."

And then halfway down the lane he turned to me in the water and said "Annie?"

I looked at him.

He said "it's your cousin Pete."

"How did you recognize me?" I said.

"It was your voice."

I was stunned and in awe and excited and would have given up my whole swim to talk to him. But after a brief chitchat he put on his goggles and said "and now we do our work-out" and he began to swim, very vigorously.

This happened two more times that summer and each time I did not recognize him. But now I seem to be accustomed to what he looks like. I think he swims at Jerry's pool a lot now, because often when Bill and I get out of the pool, he says "I saw your cousin Pete." They have long chats when they are standing up in the lane, but I don't know what they talk about.

I would see him a few times a year each summer, and I used to say "wait for me when you get out." I thought we would have cousin talk. But either he wouldn't bother to wait for me, or we would have nothing to say. And so when I saw him yesterday I didn't even try to have cousin talk, I treated him like just another swimmer in the lanes.

"All the pools are closed but this one" I said to him.

"I know" he said, "it's crowded."

"My friend Sherry told me in the shower yesterday, she came last Wednesday and it was so crowded she just took a shower and left, there were no lanes, but that was before the pools closed, maybe Wednesdays are just crowded" I said.

And then I said "I'll let you swim," and I went back to my swim.

But when we wound up at same time at end of lane, he said "have you heard from any of the cousins?" and I said "I haven't."

"I don't know anything about any of the cousins" I said, "O yes, your sister wants to be a writer, and each time I email John, he and Daisy are traveling, they went to China, then they went on long trip in the Northwest, Oregon and Seattle, and they just went back to NYC for his high school reunion. And my brother goes kayaking and takes the photos and posts them on the web and sends the link to me and my mom and all his friends."

Pete said "China! John went to China!"

"Yes, he said it was all huge construction wherever he looked."

"I guess they were putting up the Olympics" Pete said.

"I guess so, he also said none of the food was any good, he did not like one meal he had in any restaurant, and I couldn't believe he could not find good Chinese food in China."

"He should have gone to MacDonalds," Pete said.

And that made me laugh. My cousin John is a gourmet, I cannot imagine him ever going to MacDonalds, I can't imagine him even knowing what MacDonalds is.

And then we went back to our swims. And when he got out of his lane and waved goodbye, I said "can I use your lane now?" and he said "yes I am leaving." And so I had a lane of my own.

And I did not feel very related to Pete. I tried to think what was our actual family relationship, and I realized my grandparents had to be his grandparents, because his mom is my dad's kid sister. It really did seem like family when I thought we have the same grandparents, and it seemed like family when I thought his mom is my dad's sister. But it doesn't feel like family when I bump into him in the pool. I feel less close to him than I do with the other swimmers.

I see Beanie is burying his cookie. He is so serious about it. That very serious face with huge dog cookie in his mouth, as he arrives with it, and looks all around so carefully. And then all that work and effort of digging the hole for it and placing it in the hole.

I know what is cousin-like between me and Pete, we both want with all our heart for our cousin Richie to be fine. As soon as we recognized each other in pool, our first thought was "I hope Richie is fine."

And it's why I connected with my big cousin John in San Francisco to begin with, after not being in contact with him for 10 years, so we could share that feeling together of wanting Richie to be fine. We are all the cousin of Richie and we all want him to be fine. But I never reached John because he is always traveling. I guess my cousin John must be retired now, because what job lets you travel all the time?

At first I thought he was on vacation when I heard he and Daisy were in China, that was at start of summer. And then month or two later, when I heard they were on long trip in Northwest, I still thought it was John's vacation. But when they got back from that and turned right around to go to NYC for John's high school reunion, it hit me John must have retired. Altho who knows, he is a psychologist at clinic in a hospital, maybe they let him make his own hours. And Daisy has very successful catering business but maybe now it runs itself, and she can travel as much as she wants to with her husband.

I can feel a little wistful about having so little contact with my cousins, not knowing anything about their lives now, we were close as kids. I don't feel any of this about Pete, because my father's baby sister moved out here to Tucson when she was 14 years old, and married out here and had her family out here. I saw Pete way too infrequently, on those rare visits when she returned to New York City with her whole family, all 4 of her children. Pete and I did not have a relationship as children, so there is nothing to try to hold on to. There is just background. My grandparents are his grandparents. And even on his father's side, his father is a Tucson native, and his father's parents were in Tucson.

Pete said when he grew his hair long in the '60s his Tucson grandpa asked his father in Yiddish "what's up with his hair?" (Pete doesn't know any more Yiddish than I do, for him to understand this his grandfather had to say to his dad, "why is he wearing his hair like a girl?") Pete's dad talked Yiddish with his father, the way my mom had to go back to speaking Yiddish when she visited her dad in Rochester.

Here is what my Higher Self says about me and my cousins now:

When Anne decided to move to Tucson she called her cousin Pete to ask him to find them an apartment which accepted dogs, because they're flying out. By a miracle Pete found one that day, at rent Anne wanted to pay, but it turned out it only accepted dogs up to 33 pounds and Clio was 37 pounds. But it encouraged Anne no end, because she had already told her landlord she was moving and giving up her rent control apartment next month.

It turned out there were gazillion apartments for rent at what Anne wanted to pay ($300), the rub was the dog. Pete enlisted his mom's help, Anne's aunt Celia, and she found Anne a two bedroom for $330 which accepted pets. Anne said "bring the money to the manager right now, I will send you a money order to reimburse you."

And that is how the apartment was found for Anne and Bill and their dog Clio before they moved to Tucson, and her aunt put in telephone and electricity for her too. Between her aunt Celia and Pete, so many favors were done before they moved, and right after they moved (they had no car) that Anne and Bill and Clio were able to walk into their new Tucson apartment one month from the day when I had first suggested to Anne she move to Tucson, and she had decided to do it.

It is hard for Anne sometimes now to remember how close she was to all her cousins as a kid, and not feel the same closeness now. They were children then, they are not children now. She saw that when the children from family across the street came over to play in the truck her neighbor had left in her side yard. The children had a ball imagining they were all going to Disneyland together. For them the experience was real, they spent the afternoon having the trip of their dreams. But Anne just wanted to get out and go back to her computer. Her mind is in a different place now. Her cousins are all still the warm loving lively people they always were. But interests change and wavelengths change.

She feels closest to Stephen now, her cousin Goldi's husband. Because he understands where Anne is coming from. And Pete feels closer to Bill, because Bill understands him. Bill knows where he is coming from.

All Anne has to do is let go of past attachment. This means not try to force anyone to relate to her the way they related to her as a kid. But instead to see family as a dynamic living thing. Yes, her cousin Richie was her best friend as kid, but now she is friends with Stephen. They are able to sync.

If only Anne could see it's the whole secret to everything, you don't look to the past, see what it offered then, and cry because it is not now. You look in the now to see what it does offer, because that is where the gifts for you now are.

And the truth is Pete is closer to family now than Anne is. He traveled back all the way to NYC for Leon's memorial. And he went to San Francisco for the cousins' reunion Chanukah latkes party this past Chanukah. It never crossed Anne's mind to show up at that. And at her dad's memorial, sure she had loving embrace with her cousin Alley, said hi to Pete. But who did she really connect to? The mother of the girl she had been at camp with, the boy who lived in apt. 4C, and the chairman of Leon's group in the Party.

When they were lining up for food at the buffet, she couldn't resist cracking jokes with him. Then she took her food and sat down next to Marshall from apt 4C. She is the family dropout, but she won't admit it, LOL "no one wants to be close to me in the family anymore" Anne cries into her pillow. But the only dropout in this family is someone whose name begins with A and ends with E, and has two Ns in the middle. But of course Anne will never admit that in a million years.

(by Anne) Well my Higher Self is right about one thing, here is my blog about going to my dad's memorial, I found it fun to meet my dad's old friends:

The 25 Sadies (from my blog)

When my parents needed help or favors, Marshall from apartment 4C, who had stayed in the apartment he grew up in after his parents moved to Florida, was the one who helped my parents. My father had bought a digital watch and didn't know how to set it and reset it. It was Marshall who reset it when Daylight Savings began and then reset it for him when Daylight Savings ended.

When I went back home for my father's memorial, I finally got to meet Marshall, I sat next to him at the table.

My mother had rented the conference rooms in a hotel close to the airport, so everyone could get up and talk about my father, and when it was over there was a catered buffet luncheon in the next room. I sat next to Marshall, who I had heard so much about from my dad, who loved the guy so, and appreciated all his little favors.

"Yes" Marshall said, "I have it marked on my calendar, reset Leon's watch, I was looking forward to it."

Most of the people at the memorial were my father's friends from the Party. My mother was very concerned they would begin off their speeches by saying "Comrades," and use "comrades" in their speeches, because she had invited her friends from work, and she didn't want them to know about my father's political activities. She was also concerned that she wouldn't be able to recognize and identify each one of them, to give them special warm individual hello, 25 of them were named Sadie, and she was worried she would get all the Sadies mixed up.

The night before the memorial she sat with a pack of index cards with each one's name on it, and tried to memorize all the information. My father was very close to all these people and worked with them all the time, went to meetings every week. But my mother was peripherally involved, I guess she showed up with my dad at demonstrations, and possibly to other memorials, since 99 percent of them were the same age as my father.

There was only one young man my age, and I stood next to him at the buffet table putting the food on our plates. I think this young man was the president of the group, and he did say "comrades" in his speech.

"I guess Leon is up organizing in Heaven now" I said, "he probably thinks a lot of changes need to be made, and he is organizing as we speak."

"I don't think Leon believed in an afterlife" the young man said to me.

"You're right" I said to the young man. It's true my dad was atheist, but I was 100 percent New Age by that point, I knew without a shadow of a doubt that my dad was in Heaven, I had just been joking about the organizing part.

I enjoyed meeting all the alte cocker friends of my father's when they arrived, all 25 Sadies from his Party, and all the rest. Some of them had known my father from way way back. "I was in a theater group with Leon before he married your mother, when he still lived on Central Park West, we all acted in plays together."

I wasn't aware that my dad's earliest dreams involved acting and he acted in plays and had been in a theater group. My dad had been 30 when he met and married my mom, he had had a 10 year bachelor life before that. He was 7 years older than my mom, and the women who showed up for his memorial, all members of his Party, were his age, not my mom's.

One of the women said to me "I am Leslie Winnick's mother." Leslie and I had been at communist camp together when we were 12, and then at regular camp together when we were 13 and 14. I had met her at camp, and we went to camp parties together till I was 15. That is how I got to go to her apartment in Sunnyside, Queens. Sunnyside, Queens, I had become aware of from my camp friends, is where all the communists in Queens lived. Leslie had a big sister Judy, a teenager who was a counselor-in-training at the first camp I had gone to, the communist camp. I saw her at camp but I don't remember seeing her again.

Leslie was small and slender and diminutive and wore glasses, she looked like a mouse. And everyone was surprised, at the teenage work camp that we all went to when we were 14, Nancy and Leslie and Gina and me, that a huge 16 year old young man chose her for his girlfriend. Bob Levine was not only huge physically, but he belonged to such a sophisticated world. His whole life was jazz, he came into Greenwich Village to hear jazz, and he even wrote about jazz. Most of the teens at that camp went to private school and were rich. In fact the camp itself was at a private school in the Berkshires. Many of the students at that school stayed in the summer for the camp too, they didn't want to be home with their families, and I think Bob Levine was one of those.

For Leslie and me, who lived in housing projects in Queens it was another world. (It turned out to be my favorite of all the camps I went to, the people were nice, and I had a great time.)

I had a boyfriend at that camp too. He was 15, but he was small and slight, my size. He was also rich, and in that private school world. He too loved jazz, and he and Bob Levine, Leslie's boyfriend, would talk about jazz all the time. Bob Levine decided to make Leslie his girlfriend and she accepted. She had never had a boyfriend before. Neither had I actually, Fred was my first, but I was more popular at that camp than Leslie was, other boys wanted to be my boyfriend. I don't think any boy had wanted Leslie to be his girlfriend till Bob Levine chose her. I liked Bob Levine and thought he was a nice guy, I was friends with him, but I wouldn't have chose him to be my boyfriend.

At first I wouldn't make out with my boyfriend because I didn't know how to kiss, and I thought if he found out I didn't know how to kiss, he wouldn't want me, he would break up with me, and I wanted him so much. And the news that I wouldn't make out with Fred spread like wildfire around the camp. No one knew the reason why, I didn't confide to anyone it was because I didn't know how to kiss.

Most of the boys thought it was because I was a prude. Jokes were made to my face at breakfast. The boys would all say "pass the prudes, I mean prunes" and look at me and smile. Once coming back from swimming Bob Levine took me aside and solemnly explained to me it was because I was afraid of my father. I guess he knew psychology. In this camp, not only did they go to boarding school, were rich, went to jazz clubs in Greenwich Village to hear jazz, but they also went to psychotherapy. I think that was my one personal conversation with Bob Levine, he was helping me with my "problem". He and Leslie were not boyfriend and girlfriend yet, that came later.

He determined to make Leslie his girlfriend and went all out to court her. We all saw it, because at camp everything was public. And then he succeeded, she became his girlfriend. And huge Bob Levine and diminutive Leslie were always together. And then out of the blue he dumped her.

That had a terrible effect on me, because I had seen how he chose her, courted her, determined on her, won her. And then stopped wanting her and dumped her. It hadn't worked exactly like that with my boyfriend. He had been popular, all the girls wanted him, and I was one of the girls who wanted him. I was thrilled when he chose me, when he and his first girlfriend fought too much and eventually broke up. I always lived in dread that he would break up with me, and wished on every first star at night that he would keep me (or that I would keep him).

He had not gone thru any of the effort Bob Levine had gone thru to get Leslie. I assumed if Bob Levine had done all that he really wanted Leslie. It didn't add up for me at all that two weeks later he dumped her just like that. It made this whole business of having boyfriends seem so precarious to me, as if you are totally at the mercy of someone else's whim. And Leslie had liked being his girlfriend, he had treated her like a queen, and I liked seeing my friend Leslie treated like a queen. Altho Leslie and I were never close, I don't even remember one actual conversation between us, altho the 4 of us shared a room together, we had all been to camp together when we were 13, and had come to this camp together.

And here gazillion years later was Leslie Winnick's mother. I hadn't even seen Leslie since the year after camp, at the camp parties. I hadn't seen Leslie since she had been Bob Levine's girlfriend and then Bob Levine broke up with her.

"How did you remember me?" I asked when she told me she was Leslie Winnick's mother.

But I realize now she couldn't have. She had been Leon's friend all these years and in the Party with Leon, and knew me as Leon's daughter who had been at camp with Leslie.

"Leslie is in Colorado now," she told me "married and with children."

"I remember when she had that boyfriend, Bob Levine" I said.

"So do we!" she said, "we were shocked, he was such a big boy!"

I can see why Bob Levine would be shocking to parents when your daughter is only 14, and quiet little mouse with glasses. Altho I liked him and found him easy to talk to, he had big overwhelming appearance, and black rimmed glasses. He looked like a giant when he was with Leslie. He did all those romantic gestures with her when he was first courting her. I remember his reaching down and plucking a rose for her. He was like a knight from the middle ages courting a fair maiden. Altho I had no experience of affairs of the heart at that point, I still had intuition. I knew something wasn't computing right. So even tho I was deeply shocked and surprised and baffled when he broke up with Leslie, none of it from first to last had felt real to me.

I took Leslie Winnick's mother and enfolded her in my arms. You don't realize how much affection you have for your friends of yore, till you meet their mother a million years later at your dad's memorial, and the love overflows in your heart for them and for their mom.

November 21

Cars, trucks, and automobiles

There is a gentle breeze stirring everything. It even comes in and blows on my face, that coolness. It is getting stronger and more active, I wonder if it will turn into small wind.

Today is Friday so a huge event in our life takes place in two days. Bill and his friend Jim are going to the Cardinals stadium up in Phoenix to watch the Cardinals play the Giants from New York. This is such an out of the ordinary event for us that my mind is blown.

Phoenix is only a few hours away and for people who grew up in Tucson, they are always going back and forth and thinking nothing of it. They have friends who moved to Phoenix and are always going up and visiting them. They go to Phoenix at the drop of the hat.

And because Jim grew up in Tucson, he thinks nothing of it at all. He goes to Phoenix about 12 times a year. On the average of once a month he is up in Phoenix for one reason or another.

And it isn't even such a big deal for him to go to the game up there, because when he was a boy, his dad took him to professional football games up there all the time. But Bill has only been once, when his dad took him to see the Colts when he was a boy and they all lived in Baltimore.

Bill and I were up in Phoenix one time, the year after we moved here, when Ruthie called and said "the Dalai Lama is speaking in Phoenix, you have to go and see him."

And we told the people we knew then and they told their friends, and carload of us went up to see the Dalai Lama. He talked in a huge basketball stadium at a university there. He had a very thick accent, it was hard to understand him. But I remember he said one thing which was helpful to me at the time. It was a Friday I remember, and I had gotten some news from home that afternoon which had distressed my mind, I don't remember what it was. And the Dalai Lama said what he does when something distresses his mind, and so I did it and it helped.

We had only been in Tucson one year then, I still really had no idea what life was like anywhere but in New York City. I was still getting used to cars again. Of course we had a car when I was growing up, a blue Plymouth. And before that the blue Ford with the silver starter button. That had come with white walled tires and we still lived in Manhattan then and I was still little.

But the day after my dad bought the Ford, someone stole the white walled tires, so I never got to see the blue Ford with the silver starter button in its full glory with the white walled tires. But after that we drove that to the country instead of going by train and it sat in the driveway. And Richie and me and Alley and Jimmy would spend lots of afternoons sitting in the car and playing with it, playing car.

When we first moved to Tucson and let Mario keep his broken truck in our side yard, the children would come over from across the street and sit in the cab and play car in it. And I once sat there and played car with them. What we did was imagine it was driving and imagine we were going on a trip and imagine we stopped at MacDonalds and we all gave our imaginary order and ate our imaginary food. And then we went to Disneyland, of course.

The children loved it because in their mind they were living it all, having this experience. But for me then as a grown up, I wasn't. I only found it mildly interesting. But back then when Richie and me and Alley and Jimmy were little kids too, we were able to do this endlessly. Because we were able to make the experience real for ourselves.

It was very exciting when the new cars started to come in. Richie and I were slightly older now, just the right age to fall in love with cars. They were two-toned and they had fins. And the steps of our porch in the country was the perfect place to watch them all pass by on Route 28. There was no traffic on week days, but it is a resort area, on the weekends they all came up from Utica and other cities, and would pass by my porch, because Route 28 was the main drag thru the Adirondacks. I watched them all in fascination. They were so new, so modern, so shiny, the colors were so beautiful. Richie and I learned the names of all the cars, we would recognize all the cars. And I spent endless time trying to decide which one was my favorite, which I liked best.

They were all so wonderful. It could be we liked Buicks and Pontiacs best and Oldsmobiles too, and I guess I liked pink and black. Altho Richie probably liked two other colors; that they were two-toned was so much fun. My grandfather came up and visited us in his brand new green Nash. It was very exciting he had brand new car every year, but he always bought a green Nash, and Nash was not our favorite.

You couldn't get flashy enough to suit us.

And then I stopped going to the country with my family in the summers, I went to camp instead, I was teenager. And even if I went up for week or two after camp, I wasn't interested in cars, I was interested in boys. And then I moved into Manhattan with roommates, the year after high school ended. My first year at out-of- town college had not been a good experience, I transferred back to CCNY, moved in with some Barnard girls on 106th Street, and never left Manhattan again until we moved to Tucson. Cars had dropped out of my life. I could take the subway with my eyes closed, I knew it by heart. But the world of cars ended for me with those beautiful two-tones with fins, and all the car names I knew so well back then.

So naturally when we first moved to Tucson and lived in the apartment and I would take my dog Clio to Swan Park a few blocks away, I would look at all the cars parked around the park. They all looked so different now, and I couldn't recognize any of the names. They are names I am familiar with now, but not back then. Toyota and Subaru, Nissan. And when my cousin helped us buy our car a few months after we moved here, Pete had us buy a compact truck.

"I don't understand why we are buying a truck" I said to Pete, "how often are we going to haul stuff?"

"It has nothing to do with hauling stuff" Pete explained, "you buy a truck because it is a cheaper way to buy a car, trucks are cheaper than cars."

"O" I said, "O."

And he found us a great deal on a brand new red truck, it was last year's model so they had it on sale. And we bought it, and now we had one of those Japanese compact trucks like everyone else in Tucson (ours is Isuzu).

But what I found so peculiar was the front seat. When Richie and I and Alley and Jimmy had played, and the way cars were back then, you could easily fit seven in them. 3 in front seat. Altho we were so little we all squeezed in front seat. But I was used to cars where the front seat was whole long wide thing, 3 always sat in the front seat, and 4 sat in the backseat. And at first it seemed glamorous to me that it was bucket seats, only two could sit in front.

But truck has no backseat. It is very odd to me only two can sit there and you cannot give a lift to a 3rd person. I wanted to take the lady home from the grocery store two weeks ago. And Bill said "I would love to, but how can I, only two fit in, if we had the second-hand car with us, she could sit in the back, and I would gladly drive her and her groceries home."

So you can see why, a year after we moved to Tucson, and we were all going to drive up to Phoenix together, and I still didn't know cars at all, when Hank said "Great! we can all go in my car, I just bought a big new one." And he said what kind it is, but I didn't recognize it, maybe it was the first of the SUVs. And when I saw the size of it, my mind was still in cars back from when I was kid.

It was Hank and his wife Janey, me and Bill, and Mike Hurwood with his best friend, Christine. It was 6 of us, and when I was kid any car would easily have managed 7. But 1993 was another world. Only two could fit in front because of those bucket seats, so that was Hank and Janey. And only 3 could fit in back, and one person had to sit scrunched up in some back area which is meant for storage, I guess instead of trunk.

I couldn't believe a huge car like that could not carry 6 people comfortably. What is the point of such a big car then! It was very kind and generous of Mike's friend Christine to offer to be the one to sit so scrunched up in the back area. I had tried it for a while and it was so uncomfortable, so she offered to take over for me.

Christine turned out to be a yoga teacher, and was my aunt Celia's yoga teacher at the JCC. Christine also taught yoga at a fancy resort for businessmen, up in the foothills, who come here from Los Angeles to get rid of their stress. She lived in the bohemian section of Tucson on 4th Avenue (Tucson's East Village). And when I told her where I lived she wrinkled up her nose.

"Why do you wrinkle up your nose?" I asked.

"Because it is so middle class" she said.

But when I visited her and saw the view of burnt out buildings from her window, I was glad my aunt had found me apartment in middle class section of Tucson. I had lived in the East Village for 25 years, slums no longer held any charm for me. Whatever I had found romantic and thrilling and exotic and wonderful about the East Village when I first moved there, 25 years later I really had had it.

Altho it was traumatic to be suddenly plopped down in a totally middle class neighborhood in Tucson. Now I realize it is central Tucson, but when we arrived it looked like the suburbs to me. It was too alien, too different from what we were used to. We were not comfortable at all. I appreciated very much the big new clean large luxurious apartment. Not luxurious by Tucson standards, but compared to a tenement in the East Village I was wowed by the luxury, I had lived in a walk-up, my toilet had pull chain, and our apt. was teeny. This had real rooms and closets and wall-to-wall carpeting, and a normal bathroom, and a normal kitchen, and a picture window which took up one whole living room wall, and a living room.

There are no words for my amazed delight when we arrived in middle of night, turned on the lights and saw the new apartment my aunt had found for us. It was dream come true on every level, beyond dream come true, it surpassed all my dreams.

But walking around the neighborhood, altho at first we were so in love with it, eventually it was too alien. We had lived on Lower East Side too long to feel comfortable there, nothing was familiar looking. It was hard for us. And a year or two later when we discovered 4th Avenue, and downtown Tucson, where all the artists lived in old decayed neighborhoods, we said "we didn't know this existed" and "why didn't my aunt Celia move us here." It was all familiar to us. LOL we were used to old rundown decaying neighborhoods where artists lived.

Maybe we had been in the house one year when Ruthie called about the Dalai Lama and we all went up to see him. Because when I visited Christine in her apartment a few weeks later, she invited me, she was Mike Hurwood's friend, her apartment was top floor of a house near 4th Avenue. And she was the one who had wrinkled up her nose about where I live, too middle class.

Even tho Christine had nice view of the mountains from her north window, right below were all the burned out buildings on vacant lots. And it was too familiar from all my years in the East Village, and now I was used to my middle class neighborhood, I didn't want what Christine had, I wanted what we had. I had gone thru all the trauma of getting used to it, but now I liked it. I was comfortable there.

I knew Christine felt superior to me, and thought where she lived and how she lived was superior to where and how I lived. It was an attitude I had had for a long time in the East Village. But in fact my mind had changed when I was 30. It just seemed like a deprived way to live. I wanted the comforts of the middle class and I wanted the beauty of nature, but somehow I got trapped there, and didn't escape until our miraculous escape to Tucson.

And under the tutelage of my Higher Self I was learning about value versus image. Her attitude was always "try to get the best value for your money, don't pay for image, because you can manipulate image in your mind."

She placed no value on image at all. For her value meant something tangible. It is why for our second car, when my mom sent me money for driving lessons and to rent a car with an automatic, the truck had manual shift. And I saw the check was big enough to buy a second car, a used car. We went over to where we had bought the new truck and asked about their used cars.

And he said "the best value is this Chrysler 5th Avenue from 1984, the people just brought it in, to buy a brand new Buick Park Avenue instead, and it is in mint condition, altho it has a lot of miles on it."

Bill refused because it wasn't cool, but my Higher Self kept saying "Get it! it is good value, you can switch the image around in your mind later."

Which is exactly what happened. Bill caved in and we bought it. And O it was so luxurious at first. I loved it. I felt like I had a limo, it has velvet seats. Of course now it is something you would see in the trash, they were only willing to give me $100 max for it when I asked about trading it in for new car few years ago. But O I am so glad we bought it then. Because once in everyone's life, you have to have that experience of walking on velvet, of feeling like you are a very rich girl.

And my Higher Self was right about the image thing. Bill refused at first, because he said it is the kind of car all the alte cockers drive and he wants a car a 29 year old would drive. But then suddenly in the middle of our long test drive, he said "I bet this is the kind of car Frank Sinatra drives." And then we said "Dean Martin drives it! Frank Sinatra drives it! Sammy Davis junior drives it! And all the gangsters in Las Vegas!" Bill was so much happier when he decided it was car gangsters would drive, and he agreed to buy it. And I was so happy because I had my heart set on it.

I wanted that luxury, it was like having a Cadillac.

I don't even mind it that it all looks like hell now. The power windows don't work, they are all stuck somewhere in the middle. The velvet upholstery has come up. All the lining of the car, what do you call that covering, of the top on the inside, has torn away. The springs are gone in the seats, and the radio no longer works. And the air conditioning plotzed a long time ago. And of course it turned into a money pit to keep fixing the engine, it was how I was introduced to the wonderful world of car repairs. Each time something went wrong it was another $1000.

But I don't care. It was so healing after all those years of deprivation in the East Village to have this car when we did, to have that experience of having a limo. And it still looks nice from the outside, it looks like a very handsome car, it's just the inside which has turned into a shambles. The desert heat destroyed everything.

I am always grateful to Christine that both ways, she was willing to sit in that cramped back storage place when we went to hear the Dalai Lama in Phoenix. But we were not destined to become friends. I liked her and Janey, who I met for the first time too on that trip, very much, and I wanted to become friends with them and they wanted to become friends with me. But I see now it was too early in my advent in Tucson to form new friendships, they dissolved into thin air as soon as they started.

I guess everyone in the car going there was New Age in one form or another because halfway there everyone started to tell New Age jokes. Which amused me so much, I had no idea there were New Age jokes.

But after that I never tried to see the Dalai Lama again, altho Ruthie would go anywhere, any place, to see him, he meant that much to her. But struggling to understand him thru that accent, and while I was already reading *A Course In Miracles,* which was giving me everything I could possibly want to know. Ruthie and I were just on different paths.

And now 15 years later, Bill and Jim are going to Phoenix to see the Cardinals play the Giants in the big new Cardinals football stadium. They planned to rent a car at the airport for it, Jim said his car won't make it, but Bill is wondering if our second hand Chrysler would. He is going to bring it to one of the mechanics who did so much work on it and ask for an opinion.

(from my blog) **Lower East Side**

Today was a no-school holiday when I was kid. The idea of school begins off as great adventure, but somewhere along the line it changes, to just get it over. You are always waiting for time to elapse so you can have your freedom. When school finally ends you start a job. You've been in harness since kindergarten, have not known any other life.

And then maybe 10 years later or whatever suddenly you find yourself with no job. All your time is your own. The days belong to you. It is a big transition. I once heard a girl in a coffee shop, when it first happened to her, say to her friend "What am I supposed to do now? Go to a museum?"

I entered the dreamy life of my neighborhood. I would go to the Italian bread store in the morning, where the beautiful Italian girl with the big hair presided over it, and she would tell me about Priscilla Presley. And once I was in the Jewish bakery instead. And I turned around and she was waiting in line. And she turned to all the customers there and said "hahaha I caught you."

I would market in all the little stores and chit-chat with the owner and get to know him. The Italian sausage store, the Polish sausage store, the Italian bread store, the Jewish bakery, the fish store, and the dairy and cheese store.

I began to chit-chat with my neighbors. I got to know the whole world who doesn't go to work. I joined the meandering rhythms of my neighborhood. Talking to the postman as he stood in the hallway putting all the letters in the boxes. I got to know my neighborhood: the shopkeepers and the women who market. I dropped out of the professional class.

I began to realize that everyone who had stayed behind in my neighborhood, an immigrant neighborhood, were immigrants who had not bettered themselves. They all had family on Long Island and Brooklyn, and some of the owners of the stores lived there. But for the ones who were born in their tenement apartments and stayed there and lived there their whole life, the Lower East Side was home, they had never lived anywhere else. Either they had no ambition or they didn't want to leave their mother, or both.

Many had been born in the building and their mother lived in the apartment across the air shaft. The ones who never married, or for whom marriage didn't work, still lived with their mothers. I began to see their childhood in the neighborhood. There was a big step down to the feather pillow store, and to my surprise I discovered my neighbor Vie (Vincenza) when she had been toddler, would try to make that big step.

My neighbor Carmine was the oldest one. I heard from my neighbor Sal (Salvador) Carmine used to play stickball on 7th Street, but when the boys became interested in girls the stickball stopped. Sal was still younger and serious about his stickball, but Carmine and his friends stopped playing seriously. Sal said Carmine and his friends belonged to an older crowd, they were called "the old crowd," and on Sunday mornings they all went to the saloon by the Precinct on 5th Street, they would call it "going to church."

I was starting to discover where I was. Baby Vie had played on the big step on First Avenue down to the feather man's store. Carmine had played stickball on 7th Street and spent Sundays in the bar by the Precinct with his friends. Dottie and Mike had been the first ones to rent an apartment in my building after the landlord, a doctor, renovated it. It was hard to find tenants then in the '40s, and the landlord had offered them any apt. they wanted and offered to repaint the walls any color they wanted. Before landlord renovated and put in the parquet floors and French doors and in-door bathrooms, our building had had toilet-down-the-hall. "We were first building on First Avenue with in-door bathrooms" Dottie told me.

Vie was born in apartment 4A. When she and Bob married they moved to Apt 3A. After their wedding they went on the bus upstate for their honeymoon but Vie got nauseous on the bus so they turned around and came home. Vie showed me her autograph album for 8th Grade. She only got as far as 8A. On the pages the girls had written "If all the boys lived across the sea, what a good swimmer Vie would be."

Dottie's Polish priest had refused to marry her to Mike, so Dottie said "if you don't marry me I will just live in sin with Mike," so the priest did it.

Carmine referred to where he grew up as the 4th Ward. When Jimmy Durante came to visit Carmine, Carmine said "Jimmy Durante grew up in 4th Ward too." When that famous movie star who was in "Laura" walked into the pizza shop on corner of 4th Street, where Carmine hung out all day-- this is when Carmine and I were already friends but I wasn't there when it happened-- Carmine recognized his old friend from the 4th Ward and the famous movie star recognized Carmine.

"Carmine, what are you doing here" he said.

And Carmine said "let me treat you to anything you want." (Dana Andrews, that is the name of the famous move star.)

When I asked Carmine "who is your favorite movie star?" he gave the question a lot of thought.

And finally he said-- I forget his name now but it was familiar to me, I watched him recently in "The Postman Always Rings Twice." They rarely play the movies on my cable TV old-movie station which feature Carmine's favorite movie star. (I just remembered, John Garfield.)

I was learning where I was. My relationship to time changed. I was living in a stop-time place. And I got caught on a thread of history. In some ways, as the world moved forward in time, I moved backwards in time. For me personally, the world had begun on upper Manhattan, that was the world I opened my eyes to, the old A & P on Broadway.

But this world anteceded that. I realized Carmine's slang was the slang of the '30s. He didn't say "I'm broke," he said "I'm busted." He would offer me a "slug" from the bottle of whiskey I bought him in the morning. When he got back from the "saloon" I made him fried egg sandwich and coffee. He called our French neighbor Simone, "Frenchie."

It all came to a moment of finality, of apotheosis for me, about a year before I left my old neighborhood. I was on the other side of Houston Street, the real Lower East Side, it must have been around Pesach. I went to the matzo factory and bought a box of matzos there. And then for some reason I wandered into a wine store there. I saw all the wine bottles in their dark bins and knew this store had not changed one iota since the 1930s. It was April 1991 and I was in a store from the 1930s. I had reached back as far as it could go.

That was the Spring I was buying Carmine his underwear. He had sent me to the real Lower East Side to the store where he used to shop at for his sox and shorts. Maybe that is why I was wandering around there, buying the matzo at the matzo factory and walking into that old wine store, I had bought Carmine his sox and shorts and undershirts.

A lady with red hair, I forget her name now, such a nice lady, who lived with her brother on 4th Street, said "you are buying Carmine his underwear now, I used to do that for him." That was another thing about my neighborhood, how many sisters and brothers lived together. They had grown up in that apartment, and when their parents went to Heaven, sister and brother continued to live there. That lovely red haired woman and her brother were the generation of my parents, but my friend John and his sister Theresa and their brother Rick, were my generation.

I spent my first 6 months in Tucson catching up with the modern world.

November 23

Cora Leaves Phone Message

Well this is very exciting, the boys are off. Bill left to pick up Jim right now, Jim's car is not working. Then they will drive to Avis by Park Mall to rent a car. Then Bill wants to park the old Chrysler back in our driveway, so he will return, pick up the tickets for the game, and the dough I took out of bank on Friday, say good-bye to Beanie and I can kiss him good-bye.

I spent the first part of my morning looking under my bed and thru my drawers and thru my old pocketbooks looking for cigarettes. I order them on internet and in the past they always arrived 4 days after I ordered them. Now it is 16 days, and I am down to last pack. Altho I did find one whole new pack way under my bed.

I am not now so nervous that they won't arrive tomorrow evening, because when I was lying in bed last evening, I actually had a vision of the mail truck driving up and driver going in back, opening up back of truck, and taking a carton out to deliver to me. And each time I get nervous now, I remember my vision and say "they will come."

A vision is an interesting thing, and something I do not do much of, twice in New York I remember, and this one last evening of the mailman arriving and taking out package from back of truck.

What it is for me, other people may have other kinds of visions and have it more, but I saw exactly how mine worked last evening. I was just lying in bed, I had hoped the cigarettes would arrive yesterday evening and they didn't, so it was on my mind. But I was still lying in bed relaxed and happy under all those down quilts because of cold night air. And just being close to my Higher Self, not doing much of anything, no real conversation, letting my mind drift, being close to my Higher Self, being contented and relaxed.

And you know how you could see something out of the corner of your eye and not even notice it, unless you decided to focus on it. Well it was kinda like that. Instead of being at the corner of my eye tho, maybe it was from the level dreams come from, some level right below my mind, like a twilight world, definitely shades of night.

It's possible this world would go on all the time and we never notice it. It happens absolutely silently and absolutely quickly. But it was the content of it which drew my mind to it. "What did I just see?" And I realized I had seen a man at back of truck in front of my house take out a carton to bring to me. And I knew it was the mailman bringing me my cigarettes and I was so happy. And I decided to trust it. Each time I would get nervous after that, I said to myself "but you saw him delivering your cigarettes, they will come."

The vision was a gift to me.

Well Bill is back with rental car, he went into his room to get the tickets and the cash, and he told me the kitty is still sleeping on his bed, she spent the night with him, and he won't make his bed because she is nestled in so comfortably there. And so I am praying Beanie won't go in and discover her there. It is a hard place to escape from, the windows all have screens on them.

They sure got a beautiful day for driving to Phoenix. I didn't poke my head out door to see what kind of car they rented, because I was distracted about wanting Beanie not to go into room with sleeping kitty. A cat who lives outside deserves to have a night on a soft warm bed and to cuddle up with Bill. I am so glad she had that and Bill had that too.

It is so funny Bill has a cat now. But it all has to take place when Beanie and I are in other room. It is like a secret relationship we never see, which only goes on when our back is turned. The instant Beanie and I are safely ensconced in that back bedroom, kitty comes and she and Bill have whole relationship. Until Beanie and I return on the scene and she has to skedaddle and make herself scarce. Then when we go back in, she reappears again.

For past two mornings in a row and one evening in between, Cora my friend from New York City who now lives in Tucson too, has called me to tell me to listen to the program she is listening to on the public radio station. The first time she called she was surprised at the abrupt way I answered the phone. But I was already outside and had rushed in, and assumed it was Jim of course, he is the only one who ever calls me.

I just said one loud "hello," because he is always on cell phone driving. And it was Cora and she was taken aback by that greeting, and I was surprised it was her. And she said "I don't have any time now, but they are playing the most beautiful jazz." And I thanked her and we got off.

The next phone call came in from her at 9:30 in the evening, and I was in back bedroom with Beanie, and I wasn't going to rush in to answer the phone. Because Priscilla, that is the name Bill gave his cat, was in the kitchen with Bill, they were discussing her supper. Priscilla likes 3 suppers, one right after the other. No way was I going to go charging thru the kitchen with Beanie at my heels, to get to phone in my computer room. And then this morning Cora called again to tell me Maya Angelou is reading the poem she wrote for her daughter. And our conversation was just one minute, but I was able to be sweeter to her.

And yesterday afternoon I remembered that phone call which had come in the evening and clicked the answering machine to hear it. It was Cora to tell me what was on the radio now. But because she had reached my answering machine, she expanded herself. And after she told me what was on the radio now she talked a little about herself.

She asked what was I doing for Thanksgiving, and she is going to her sister Marta's house, and she told me Marta has moved, Marta is now living on 6th Street near

Speedway. And Marta didn't have Thanksgiving last year and Cora doesn't know why and will ask her. And how am I? And she hopes I am fine.

And maybe I need money and she wishes she had money for me, and maybe she owes me money? And she sent all her love to all of us and that "includes the furry four footed friends" she said, meaning our dogs, how can she know about Priscilla.

It was a very sweet very loving phone message and very satisfying to hear. We had been best friends a long time ago. In fact I was remembering in bed later that evening the friendship must have started around same time as Woodstock, because I borrowed Cora's sleeping bag for Woodstock. We must have just met around then, and she offered her sleeping bag when I said I want to borrow one.

I realized later, when Cora had opened up by saying "I can't stay on the phone, I have to get ready to leave for an appointment," that this was a night phone call, not a morning phone call, so the appointment Cora was getting ready for, it was to go over to her lover's house, she was going over for an evening of love making. I am sure she has the same boyfriend.

And because she talked to me so lovingly in her long phone message, it made her sound so sane. We had had a very long conversation on the phone one Sunday morning last year, and when it was over I wondered if my dear friend Cora had gone a little cuckoo. But love and sanity must be the identical thing. Because every word in her phone message, every intonation of her voice, breathed her love for me. And as a result the whole phone message was crystal clear sanity. It was a completely sane mind expressing itself on my answering machine. It was nice to be back in touch with Cora's sanity and love.

And she really did pick out the things I would have liked to hear, if I wanted to be listening to the radio instead of what I was doing then. I would have liked to hear the most beautiful jazz in the world. I would have liked to hear Maya Angelou reading the poem she had written for her daughter.

Even tho Cora and I have had so little contact since she moved to Tucson, two phone calls and that is it. And so little contact our last ten years together in New York, three phone calls and that is it. When was the last time Cora and I had a real ongoing friendship, it could be 27 years ago or more. There is an Anne in her mind, the Anne she knows and keeps in her mind, which is very true to who I am. In fact for a long time Cora knew me better than I knew myself, I am only recently catching up to knowing the Anne that Cora has always known.

I think that is wonderful and special about my friendship with Cora. When you are with a friend you always do encounter the person they think you are, because who they relate to is who they think you are, and how they relate to you is based on that.

And Cora has always related to me with such sweetness and lovingness, has always seen me as "dear Anne." I know she relates to everyone that way, because Cora sees everyone as sweet and loving. But that is Cora's great strength. She sees into everyone's soul, how sweet and loving they are, and that is all she sees, and all she relates to. This is why it doesn't matter how many times Cora has appeared to go off the beam, she always returns to perfect sanity. It's because of her pure loving heart, and because that is all she sees in everyone she encounters....

I giggled when I remembered Cora saying "I may owe you money." She owes money to everyone in the whole world. But the statute of limitations has given out on that ages and ages and ages ago. Which proves I guess how transient money really is when you come right down to it. It is a thing of the moment, a temporary fleeting thing, because here are Cora and I, who first became friends obviously the day before Woodstock, and the love between us is as timeless, as eternal, as powerful and real, as it ever was. It is unchanged, so big and deep it fills the universe. Whereas the 40 or 50 dollars (I have no idea the amount now) that changed hands between us back then, they are like the autumn leaves which fell and turned into dust so many seasons ago, lifetimes have taken place in the interim. They have turned into 3 dust particles in Cora's mind and that is all...

My friendship with Cora is a footnote in my life now, but once it was a blazing star of love which shed its light over my whole life. I was living with Bill. He was working as Wall Street messenger by day and going to school at night. Cora visited every evening while Bill was studying at the big teacher's desk in other room. I was 25, Cora was 24.

from my blog **Gurus and Companions**

Today is Jeannie's birthday. Ruthie's birthday was last week, Cora's birthday is next week. And my 3 friends named Pam have their birthdays at this time. Pam my friend at college, Pam who used to talk on phone about astrology with me back in NYC, and Pam at the swimming pool who got me back into writing. My Moon is in this astrological sign. These women have been paths for me. Cora opened up the greatest path for me, love and spirituality. And Ruthie took me further along that path. Jeannie taught me women's liberation and art. My friend Pam in college taught me intelligence. You could say they were all my gurus, they were my teachers.

The teaching styles were very different. Cora arrived at my apt. every evening, sat at my kitchen table while I made her coffee, and asked for my advice and told me all her problems. No one had ever asked for my advice before. I was famous for being an idiot, a chicken without a head. People would say "I worry about you, Anne."

Everyone saw me as a mess. But not Cora. We'd have coffee, she'd settle down happily and tell me the long stories of her problems. At that time she was still trying to hold a job, so most of it had to do with jobs. She was a waitress at Wall St. lunch counter when she accidentally dropped the piece of luscious chocolate cake the man had been eyeing on his lap. She was in the typing pool when the woman kindly and gently and lovingly took her aside and explained she has to be fired because she arrived 3 hours late at work every day.

In Cora's world everyone was an angel. She saw everyone thru a loving empathetic lens. She had such sympathy for her landlord, Mr. Kessler. Each month Cora would arrive with five dollars to pay down on the rent she owed from 4 months ago, until Mr. Kessler couldn't take it anymore, and said "Cora let's start from scratch." Mr. Kessler was a saint to put up with this the whole time Cora lived there. She did not get evicted until the neighborhood changed and landlords were offered big money for their tenements. As Cora explained to me, "having another de-rent controlled apt. sweetened the deal." Cora was evicted from her rent controlled apt. where her rent was only $70 per month. She was 6 months behind at that point.

Because Key Food closed at 9 pm, at few minutes to 9 she would put on her coat and all her scarves, and say "thank you dear sweet Anne" and look at me with face of such love, and try to get to Key Food in time to bang on the doors and get them to open for her. "Is there anything you want at Key Food she would ask?" So sometimes she would return with something I needed.

Compared to Cora the official story that Anne is such a mess I realized was not quite true. I was able to keep my job. I was able to pay my rent. I paid my electricity too. When we had the big black out, Cora was reading by a candle. She looked outside when she heard all the noise and saw the streetlights were out. "Why are they making such a fuss about the streetlights being out," she thought, and went back to reading by her candle. She didn't know electricity had gone off for the city.

But what I learned from Cora was everything. I learned from Cora that all people are angels and I am an angel too. Before that I thought all people were monsters and I was a monster too. I had no idea you could see people thru the eyes of peaceful love, and as a result see yourself that way too. Cora used to refer to herself that way. She would refer to her own sweetness. And I, who had always hated myself, was floored that Cora loved herself. And she saw me thru such loving appreciative eyes. I began to see myself that way too. You could say Cora liberated me. She did.

Cora was a good antidote for me for my friendship with Jeannie which had preceded it. What ruined that friendship was my intense envy. At first I just whole-heartedly admired Jeannie and I expressed all my admiration. I was happy admiring her and expressing it and she was happy to be admired. But then she wrote a book it got published she became famous, and I became very envious of her.

Before she wrote her book she had been a painter. It was my first introduction to the world of art, and to the life of a working artist. It caused a great switch in values for me. I had never considered anything other than the professions before. In fact I was school teacher during our friendship. Jeannie was quite contemptuous of the professions. "Women are always shoved into the helping professions" she announced at a women's liberation meeting.

In our personal friendship I saw how much art gave her. For Jeannie art gave her everything. "An artist's childhood is their treasure chest" she told me, "it is what the artist draws from." Because of Jeannie I wanted to become a writer, I wanted it with all my heart. And it had never occurred to me to want it before. It had not even occurred to me I could do it before. I thought you had to have talent. But Jeannie had said "the best painter in art school said 'there is no such thing as talent.'" She said the other girls in art school made their own clothes, did crafts, and did other things. "They spread themselves too thin" Jeannie told me, "you have to just do your painting in order to be good at it."

Ruthie was my best friend when my big troubles arrived. She taught me that prayer works, and also she got me to consider Jesus which is why I opened up the New Testament and read "The Gospel of St John" when I was so frightened my beloved dog would not make it. The spiritual path I am on now came from Ruthie.

But I would never have been open-minded to spirituality at all were it not for Cora. Cora's solution when things got very bad, which they always did, was to pray. That is how she balanced herself. She had a moment when the landlord had evicted her and all her stuff was on the street, when she lost her balance. But she prayed to Mary, and she regot her balance. Mostly Cora prayed to God, she said "the Father is stronger than the Son" but at times of extreme crisis, and her whole life was crisis, she would remember her mother's words about Mary and ask Mary for help.

I, who never had any balance, watched Cora hold on to her balance no matter what was thrown at her. And finally asked "How do you pray Cora? Do you just ask God for what you want?"

"No Anne" she said "you thank God for already giving it to you."

I didn't begin to pray till my time of great troubles arrived and Ruthie said "prayer works." But it is from praying that I first found out God is real. Everything else stemmed from that. I would be totally desperate and then I would remember about praying. And at first I would think "what good will praying do? I won't believe God is real till He sits down next to me and smokes a cigarette with me." But I was so desperate I would pray anyway. And always to my amazement I would find I was calmed down from it.

Irene was my companion during my great travails. She was born in October, she wasn't one of my teachers like the other girls. We learned from each other. Our friendship consisted of communication. We would share experiences and see what we learned from it. We were partners learning spirituality together. We had the same problems at the same time and we learned from each other.

Gurus matter but so do learning partners. You learn from gurus from the examples they set. I learned from Cora from Jeannie from Ruthie by watching them. Irene is how I learned from my own experience. You have to have someone to share your experience with to make it real.

My last friend before I left NYC was Marjorie. We would walk our dogs together, or she and I and my dog would walk to Delancy Street for her to place her bet at OTB. Her husband Joe did not follow the horses but Marjorie said he had genius with numbers. She would place the bet for him, and they would always win. I did not know about the winning. Finally after doing it for months, walking with her to Delancy Street, I said "why do you bet Marjorie?"

She said "people assume betting means you lose money but Joe wins."

It never occurred to me anyone ever wins, I thought betting was way to lose money. You could say Marjorie taught me about gambling.

I'm trying to think what I learned from Marjorie and it doesn't seem like very much. Once I wore a black T shirt and she said "you look good in black Anne." Mostly I loved Marjorie because I loved being with her. I just found everything she said interesting. We both took out lots of library books. She said "it is the women in the Agatha Christie mysteries who are so interesting." She read books about everyone, rock stars, everyone. She said "I am like Joe Friday, 'just give me the facts, Ma'am.'" She read a biography of Jim Morrison of "The Doors" and talked about it a lot, so I read it too.

Marjorie was a painter too.

"What do you paint Marjorie?"

"I just paint paintings of people committing suicide" she said. Marjorie had tried to commit suicide. She went to flea bitten hotel and took pills. But Joe, who was her boyfriend then, found her and took her to Bellevue and had her stomach pumped. He saved her. Marjorie used to say "I don't know what to do with the rest of my life, I never expected to live past 30."

Marjorie and I were both working as part time secretaries for psychiatrists. Marjorie said "I see the patients when they walk in, they are so upset, and then I see them when they leave, they are so calmed down." She had so much respect for the psychiatrist she worked for.

Marjorie cared passionately about the Mets and the Yankees. She would listen to the games on the radio as she painted. In some way Marjorie is the most like Bill, not only because they are passionate sports fans, but because from each of them I got to be in another world. Marjorie was born in July, she is not the same astrological sign as my gurus, and she was not a guru, she was a friend.

Our friendship fulfilled itself after I moved to Tucson. I would write to Marjorie but she never wrote back. Finally after a few years she wanted to argue with an astrological insight I had sent her. "I don't know how to write a letter" she said "I never wrote one before, but I will try to do what you do," and she wrote back.

By then I was totally with my Higher Self so I would write her my experiences with my Higher Self. And after a few months of this, Marjorie connected to her Higher Self too. So we shared our experiences with our Higher Self. We wrote to each other every single day for 6 solid years, sharing our daily life and our experiences with our Higher Self. We each knew every single detail of each others daily life.

And then Ruthie taught me how to be on internet and I never wrote another letter again. I always hoped Marjorie would understand. I guess I thought she would, because what I learned from Marjorie was understanding.

November 24

I talk to Simone on the phone in New York City

I was up at dawn, I heard the bird whistle in her nest. Sun has not yet risen above mountains. Altho the top of that tree to my west is that dusky gold it turns when first of sun's rays hit it.

I woke up betwixted and bewildered. LOL all my habits and routines got disrupted yesterday. We didn't go swimming because Bill and Jim went to Phoenix to see the game. I had to ration my last pack of cigarettes which meant I never knew what I should be doing, because everything I like to do involves smoking. I would have posted on internet more but that involves smoking, so I went in to lie down and read a book. But instead of reading book I turned on the TV. I had not watched TV in a month, ever since I discovered I could buy paperbacks for 50 cents at the charity bookstore. TV actually worked out. The first show I watched was Ralph Kramden running for Assemblyman from Brooklyn. It was completely wonderful to turn on TV after not watching it for a month and there is Ralph and Alice and Norton and Trixie, and Ralph campaigning for votes. I never saw that show before, and of course now elections and politics are center stage in my life. And after that PBS had a special about Alistair Cooke, and I found that very interesting to watch, and Bill came home in the middle of it.

He said "it was great game even tho the Cardinals lost, it was an exciting game, and they had to park in parking lot so far away, but free buses took them to the stadium, and they arrived just in time for kick-off. And the food in stadium is 15 dollars for sandwich, but Jim who knows Phoenix like the back of his hand took them to a place where they got prime rib sandwiches for $3.95." Bill said there is a retractable roof, but they kept the roof on because Phoenix was warm yesterday afternoon, so the result is "it was like watching game in a huge shopping mall, except it was so much more crowded and there was so much more noise and they played loud rock and roll."

I said "would you go back next year?" and he said yes he would, so I guess he did like it. Everything seemed to work. The tickets I had printed up on internet worked fine, the seats were fine "very high up but on a diagonal and Jim had brought his binoculars." Bill seemed satisfied.

My big news was that in the middle of the afternoon (while Bill was at game) I had called my neighbor Simone in New York. When the voice on the answering machine was the voice of a man I did not recognize, I assumed her phone number had been changed. So instead of saying "this is Annie in Tucson, your neighbor from 81 First Avenue," just in case it actually was Simone's answering machine, I just said "Simone, this is Annie," and I left my phone number.

I didn't think Simone would call me back, even if it was her number. But I guess I had gone in to read, it was early in the afternoon, and dozed off, and when I came to I heard a phone ringing, and I wondered who it was. And I did rush in and it was Simone. I was so surprised! And she said she listened to the phone message two times to figure out who I was, and finally she did, and she was glad to talk to me.

Of all the old neighbors, only 3 are left in the building. Vie is there, Simone is there, and Don upstairs. Simone and Vie are very close and she helps Vie out. She said her daughter Amy is married and lives in Brooklyn now, I didn't find out what her son Roy is doing. She said she has a website and her paintings are up on her website.

And I asked about Arthur and Hiroko, who used to live next door to her with their little girl, but who moved to Ojai California about 6 years before I moved to Tucson. Simone and Hiroko remained best friends, they are both artists and Hiroko would stay with Simone each time she came to New York.

In fact Hiroko was staying with Simone the morning we left for Tucson. I had some pretty little beaded evening purses Irene had given me and I brought them in to see if Simone or Hiroko wanted them. Hiroko did. Plus I also brought Simone my plants. I had so many beautiful avocado plants growing on my fire escape then, and I brought them all in for Simone. I gave Vie my pink begonia, and Simone said "why didn't I give that to her too, she always wanted a pink begonia." I gave Don one of my huge avocado plants too.

Hiroko's little daughter was only 3 or 4 then but I realized she must be young woman now. And when I asked Simone on phone yesterday she said "funny you should mention Arthur and Hiroko because she hasn't thought about them for years, they are still in Ojai, but their daughter came to New York recently, so Simone saw her, their daughter is now 24 years old."

It wasn't that easy talking to Simone on the phone. I understood her French accent, but whether it was because she was on cell phone or because of the language thing, everything seemed to be miscommunication.

When I said "Hiroko's daughter must be young woman now," Simone thought I was talking about her daughter and said "yes she is married and living in Brooklyn."

When I said "I wanted to call you and decided I would when Bill went to the game with his friend in Phoenix," Simone heard that as "Bill moved out, is no longer living with me, and lives with his aunt."

It took 3 whole conversations to say "Bill and I are still here together in our house."

Simone said she bought a house in North Carolina on the beach and it was the best thing she ever did in her life. I had known that from a previous conversation 5 years ago, but back then I found out she didn't live in her house, she just rents it out.

So when I said "you rent it out?"

She said she goes there and goes to the beach.

She said her apartment in New York turned out to be a treasure because she is in the middle of everything and her rent is still low because of rent control.

She said "everyone else in the building now moves in for a year and then they move out again, no one stays."

I am sure the rent is sky high, there is no reason to stay. Only she and Vie and Don are on rent control.

She said she has a website now and all her paintings are up on her website. There are about 30 of them and she will send me the address on email, and her email address is Simone at gm.com.

And I never heard of gm.com as an email address, but I wrote it down. And luckily at end of the conversation I said "your address is GM.com? like General Motors?" And she said "no! gmail.com" and that made more sense.

The conversation did not get interesting till we talked about politics. We both danced around each other, each assuming the other was still a left-winger, but then it turned out we both said "Sarah Palin is a breath of fresh air." Simone said "I was liberal and Democrat my whole life but now I am changing, I am almost a Republican." And I said how I have changed a lot too. And she said "a lot of the artists in New York have."

And I was surprised at this. Simone said "you must have heard about the big shift, the planet is in a new place now, and as a result people are no longer left and right, everything is in the center now."

I wondered if Simone knew about the Planetary Awakening in 2012 but I was afraid to introduce ambitious topics. Because when I said "Bill is a painter now and was in an art show," she thought I said "Bill moved out and lives with his aunt." And when I asked about Hiroko's daughter she thought I was asking about hers. I thought if I said "have you heard about the planetary awakening," we would misunderstand each other for 20 minutes before we got near talking about the same thing.

I was amazed we were able to click talking about Sarah Palin, we saw eye-to-eye about her, and that was gratifying to both of us and big surprise to both of us. Simone said she is tired of arguing about her, "so many people say bad things about her." She said "you know what New York is like."

I said "yes New Yorkers are emotional."

She said "yes, so much fighting about politics."

She said "I am sure it is not like that where you are, it is like that here because everyone lives in tiny apartment, is so intense."

I understand Simone's mindset because I used to be a New Yorker. She assumes that everything is different everywhere else. She doesn't realize it is the same everywhere, that there is no boundary. She thinks there is a boundary around New York City, and in the City it is one way and outside the boundary it is all completely different.

But this boundary exists in her mind, not in reality. The same thoughts feeling emotions intensities and fights about politics are taking place everywhere.

Simone said everything is fine for her now but she could use a little more money and I said "it is the same with me, all is fine, but I wish I had more money."

She said "this financial thing is scary."

I said "some prices are going down, things are very affordable, a new computer now is S250 and flat screen monitor is $150."

And she said "prices are going down for you but here in New York everything is going up, food has become very expensive, it's where you are that prices are going down."

But again, this is her idea that New York is one thing and rest of country is something else. Because the new computer and flat screen at Office Depot which is so affordable, all she would have to do is click on Office Depot on her computer, and order it, and it would come right to her at the same price.

And then she said she is on cell phone and the minutes are expensive and I had thought weekends were free for cell phone, so I said "of course I understand." She said "email me, we will do all our talking on email." And we each gave each other our emails.

Last time Simone gave me her email at Yahoo she never answered any of my emails, but maybe she is a real email person now. If she is on cell phone and the minutes are expensive, maybe she has switched to email. It would be nice to continue conversation with Simone on email.

A neighbor in tenement building in New York, where you share a wall, and the walls are paper thin, means you know their whole life and they know your whole life. For the whole time you live there you hear all their conversations on the phone, they hear all of yours.

They hear you in the kitchen, you hear them. You heard them giving their little boy his bath when he was 3 years old, you heard the police call when the boy is wild at 16, saying "he is at the precinct come get him!" You pass each other on the steps five times a day. And each time Simone got something new, she called me in so I could see it. It's a totally intimate way to live. For the whole time we were neighbors, we knew every intimate detail of each others life. There was no way not to.

I shared my other wall with Vie and the result was Vie and I knew each others life too. But her life had no drama in it, was not like Simone's and mine. Vie's life was, she would come back with her grocery shopping and take everything out of the bag and call out to her husband in bed what she bought and how much it costs. And then she would read out everything which was on TV, and then they would watch TV. And I would know what was on from what she called out. And sometimes I would just listen in to the show thru the wall, and hear them laughing. They loved their favorite shows.

I watched Simone's daughter and son grow up. Amy was about to turn 8 and Roy was about to turn 3, when they all moved in. And when I left Amy was already living with her boyfriend in the East Village and was about to move to Phoenix with him. And in fact, soon as we moved into the Tucson house the following year, Simone was up in Phoenix visiting her daughter and her boyfriend. She called me from Phoenix and said "Amy took her to Sedona and Sedona is beautiful."

But Amy didn't stay in Phoenix, she moved to California, and then moved back to New York City. And is no longer with the same guy she was with since she was 15 years old. Roy was always getting pulled in by the cops just before I left, but it was before he was 18, so all Simone had to do was come to the Precinct around the corner and get him. But he is 30 now and everything worked out perfectly, altho I didn't get to ask what he is doing now.

Of course I would love to hear all about Amy and Roy, I know them since they were children. I even remember when Amy turned 12 and that big change started. Instead of being involved in roller blades she was involved in washing her hair. And I was so interested she went out and bought Breck shampoo for the big era of hair-washing which launches our teenaged years. Breck shampoo was what I bought when I launched my hair-washing which launched my teenaged years. It was the first time I went to the drug store and chose my own shampoo for my own hair instead of using the family shampoo in the family shower. My mother must have bought some big jug of castile soap which she poured into a ketchup bottle (the kind on the Formica tables in coffee shops) and everyone used that. But when I wanted to be beautiful at 12 years old I went and bought myself Breck shampoo and washed my hair all the time with that. It all begins with washing your hair, and it all begins with Breck shampoo....

I didn't want to put in this chapter about Simone (as I was writing it) the reason we are so close, because I didn't want to remember the turmoils we both went thru at the same time, during those years leading up to me leaving New York. But I'm glad I changed my mind and talked about it in my blog. Because it makes it more real, about Simone and me. What we shared and what we mean to each other:

(from my blog)
Simone and I are now emailing

Simone was my next door neighbor the whole time I lived at 81 First Avenue. We shared a wall together and heard each others whole life. When I sent her the last story I wrote few days ago, the part she responded to in the story was how I stopped at Walgreen's on way home to buy new nail polish. She wrote back

WOW you are wearing nails polish? i am surprised you would do that in the Bundoock, or maybe you have a very social life or just having fun or bored or plain sophisticated? LOL

And for some reason yesterday afternoon I emailed back about the nail polish. I said "you introduced me to nail polish Simone and I have been wearing it ever since, I love it. And I dress differently in Tucson than I did in New York. I wear skirts and tops, not jeans, and most of my skirts have ruffles on them, and they are all summer clothes and pretty."

In fact in New York I dressed in rags. I don't know why? It was a habit I fell into and once I fell into that habit I stayed there.

But in Tucson my Higher Self wanted me to shop to buy pretty clothes, to buy new clothes and to dress pretty and so I have. And it turns out to be very good idea for me. It really lifts my spirits and adds tingle to life, like seltzer, makes it more bubbly and elated, adds oomph. I like wearing new pretty clothes now.

After I wrote Simone that little email about wearing nail polish all the time, it makes me happy, and how I dress differently in Tucson, it makes me happy, I decided I would find the tiny little story I wrote two years ago before I was on email with Simone about my last day in New York and leaving New York for Tucson. I thought she would enjoy reading it. She is a part of that story even tho she is not in it. I spent my last morning in New York in Simone's apartment. I had brought in all my house plants to give her, also to tell her I was moving to Tucson that day.

Hiroko was there visiting. I lived in apt 3B, Simone was in apartment 3C, she shared her other wall with apartment 3D which is where Arthur and Hiroko had lived when they lived in New York. Then Hiroko had a baby girl, and then Arthur got a teaching job in Ojai California and they moved there. But we all stayed close with them, me by mail, and Hiroko (who was a painter like Simone) would sometimes come to New York and stay with Simone. Altho sometimes the whole family came in. And when I brought in my house plants and to tell Simone I was moving to Tucson, that day Hiroko was there, she was staying with Simone visiting. I brought in the tiny little very pretty evening bags Irene had given me and gave them to Hiroko and she loved them.

And I guess that was the last time I saw Simone. We were on the phone quite a bit when I first moved here, but really not that much, maybe 5 short phone calls. Our relationship was neighbors, not on the phone. We saw each other 20 times a day on the steps or in front of the house or in her apt. or mine, but we had never had a telephone conversation before.

And our conversation when we saw each other was mainly "show and tell." She would show me the new thing she bought for her apartment or the new nail polish she was wearing, or her new perfume. I would see her outfit and how pretty it was and comment. Simone never wore jeans, only pretty skirts and pretty tops. Really our whole relationship was about clothes. We both love clothes. And of course nail polish, perfume, and lipstick, which we both love. Altho Simone wears all of the above, and at the time I just dressed in rags.

The other half of our relationship was the unseen half. Which was that the wall between us was paper thin, so we each heard each others whole life. So really we were more like sisters, each having our own room, and our own parallel lives. She had her friends and I had mine. Altho there was one friend we shared, Micheline. And I guess Hiroko. Altho Hiroko was much closer to Simone than me. And I guess Randi who moved in when Arthur and Hiroko left. But Randi became best friends with Simone, whereas Randi and I had small bud of friendship. But Simone and I shared all the neighbors, and in our tiny tenement all the neighbors were very close. Most of the other neighbors had been born in their apartment and grown up there. They were part of the immigrant wave to the lower east side.

After our 5 phone calls our first year, my first year in Tucson, I rarely talked to her. Occasionally when I wanted to buy a gift for my mom-- since Simone always wore expensive French lipstick, I would call up and ask "What shade are you wearing now? What do you love most?" And she would say the Dior shade she is wearing for winter and the Dior shade she is wearing for summer now. And I would find an expensive department store in Tucson which sold fancy French lipsticks and buy both for my mom.

But that was ages ago. And then when Bill and Jim were up in Phoenix for the game, my Higher Self suggested I call her. I didn't recognize the voice on her answering machine, I thought maybe she had moved to North Carolina, I had found out she bought a house on the beach there. But I left a message anyway. I didn't expect her to call me back. There was some point when we each obtained the other's email address and she never emailed me back. But to my absolute shock, she did call me back, and we had a really nice conversation, and we gave each other our new emails. And this time email took. We do correspond on email.

It was so close to the election when I called her, maybe a week after it, that we each summoned up our courage and told each other our politics had changed, and we were both amazed we both see things the same way now. That made a very close bond. Because in the circles Simone moves in New York, and with me with all my old New York friends, how Simone and I see politics now is taboo. It is grounds for being an outcast. We are "one of them" instead of "one of us" -- the awful evil people, the dullards and the despised by all sophisticates and intelligentsia, the trailer trash redneck contingent. Which is so funny considering that Simone is a little French girl, and I am a little Jewish New Yorker whose parents were Reds, a bona fide red diaper baby. And Simone comes from the French aristocracy originally, altho she and I became hippies in the '60s, even tho she was still a stewardess then for the French airlines. I don't think Simone was from high up aristocracy, her dad worked for French NATO, and Simone grew up in Morocco, her dad was stationed there. But her parents went to all the balls and dinners at the French embassy, it was classy life.

But in New York she met Geoffrey, who had a nice life back then and was a photographer. They moved to the French countryside and had their two children, I guess they married there. And then came back to live next door to me.

When I met them it was a just quick stop-over. Geoffrey's sister had found and rented the apartment for them, they were en route to New Mexico.

But it is almost 30 years later and Simone is still in that apartment, her daughter is married and living in Brooklyn, I don't know where her son is now, he was two years old when they moved in. Geoffrey's life in New York did not work out. Eventually Simone forced him to leave. And the last I heard he was living in Woodstock. But Simone told me on the phone he is now in Heaven. Which is OK, Geoffrey refused to make a life for himself when his wife kicked him out. He was always completely in love with Simone, he always wanted Simone. He chose to sink into a life of misery when he couldn't have her, it is better he have all the happiness Heaven offers, the world held nothing for him without Simone.

But I think that is a part of our tremendous closeness now, I mean the sisters aspect between us. We each lived thru with each other all the trials and tribulations our marriages went thru at the same time. We each heard it thru the walls and saw it happening for both of us. Simone and I have no secrets because we each were witnesses to everything the other went thru. And you could say as a result we each know each other's strength. Simone had to rebuild her life from scratch without Geoffrey and I had to rebuild my marriage from bottom up. We each rebuilt our lives from bottom up and we each saw the other doing it.

But any time we attempted to be regular friends, to share thoughts with each other, it never worked. We were never able to click. Which is odd, because we each clicked with Randi, with Hiroko, with Micheline, but we never clicked with each other.

But we did click on the phone after the election when we talked about politics. We each were amazed we saw it all the same way. Isn't that interesting. It is politics which has brought me and Simone together as friends. Now we email together like regular friends.

Our first emails

It is new and wonderful that now Simone and I email as regular friends about anything and everything. I am learning her delightful sense of humor, and her ideas too, which interest me.

But it goes without saying if I am finally on email with my French neighbor back in New York I am going to ask her for her new beauty tips first. So I share these below:

(Simone) WOW you are wearing nails polish? i am surprised you would do that in the Bundoock, or maybe you have a very social life or just having fun or bored or plain sophisticated? LOL Thanks for the great writing! When are you publishing with Knofp?

(Annie) Hi cookie
You introduced me to nail polish back in front of 81 First Ave when you showed me your nails and said "look at this beautiful red!" (it was Cherries in the Snow)
You said "Revlon makes beautiful nail polish"
So I went out and bought it, and have been wearing nail polish ever since. I love it, you did me great favor
Now I have so many different color nail polishes, I have too many!
Maybe I will start wearing perfume and lipstick too, which is your favorite perfume now? your favorite lipstick?
I don't dress in rags anymore, I like wearing pretty clothes on the desert, all my clothes are pretty now, and yes I shop a lot
I look for clearance in the Department Stores, and try to find pretty stuff on it
I don't wear jeans or shorts, I like skirts, and yes I have a lot of ones with ruffles, I like ruffles
O Simone, you would be proud of me, I finally learned how to dress!
LOL I have no social life here, altho I have some nice friends
I prefer to socialize on the computer

I email with friends, and also I am on a political/news forum
altho I love to chat with people at swim pool or in stores
I love you, Annie

Dear Annie,
I remember the scenario of the nail polish very well!
No more lipstick for me any more! Now I use a mat stick that i love called "Bahama" by Nars.
You can use it on the lips, on the cheeks, eyes, very versatile! And Mat like velvet and doesn't bleed!
Bahama is color pink prune toward blue not orange!
I also wear eventually essential oils, i love Geranium! And Neroli!
Write to you tomorrow!
love you simone

November 25

Coach Lisa

Well Lisa is proud of me. When she originally emailed me about novel-in-a-month I thanked her out of politeness. But she emailed back "so are you going to do it?" And I think I left that email unanswered. Then she arrived with the book from Bookman's (Bookman's is our second-hand bookstore) by the founder of novel-in-a-month, on how to write a novel in a month. Lisa had read it and highly recommended it. I thanked her very much. But when she said "the sales slip is with it in case you want to return it for another book," my eyes gleamed.

This was the week before the big election, my mind was totally taken up with that. I would just go on the computer to read election news, or talk about it with fellow posters on my news forum. However I had made the great discovery that the charity bookstore on way home from pool had used paperbacks for 50 cents. I hadn't read a book in ages and ages because library is really out of our way, I was totally starved for reading. Without anything to read, my whole life when I was not on computer, was TV shows. Until I discovered there was a way for me to read books again, which was about a month before Lisa told me about novel in a month.

I began by buying every Agatha Christie they had, even tho I had read them all a long time ago, it was long enuf ago. O I loved them so much, reading was such a joy and those were the perfect books to read. I was so happy to be reading again. The first few times I only bought mysteries at the charity store, but the third time I went I noticed the paperback mysteries were in the same section as the classics and I bought *Sense and Sensibility* by Jane Austin. And after I finished all the mysteries and there was nothing left to read, I opened up *Sense and Sensibility* and began to read that. At first I found it unreadable. I would try to read a little and then put it aside in frustration, "this is torture" I said. But then I got used to her writing and I got caught up in the story, and I enjoyed what I was reading, and sometimes it was very funny. I got completely addicted. I really loved that book. I am sorry it ended. And this is what I had just begun reading when the month of November arrived.

I was spending my mornings at computer with election news, and the afternoons and evenings with *Sense and Sensibility*, the story of Elinor and Maryanne, two sisters, when England was still very rural, it was how the gentry lived.

I had decided I would do Novel-in-a-month, why not! It would bring me back to writing again, and it was an unknown and an adventure. And I told Lisa I would start a day or two after the election. I couldn't imagine starting before, my whole mind was on the election. Lisa tried to convince me to start on November first the way you are supposed to, "surely the election cannot take up the whole of your mind!" she emailed me. But I still had it in my mind the election was Tuesday, so I would start on Wednesday.

Meanwhile I guess Lisa decided to do it herself. She had read the book by the founder of Novel In A Month. She had always wanted to write. She was a painter and had been to art school but she always wanted to write. And the founder had explained this is a good way to start writing. And he is right about that. It's a great way to start writing. This is a huge favor to anyone who has ever dreamed of becoming a writer.

That made it a whole lot more fun that Lisa and I were going to do it together. I never had a writing partner and companion in that way. I loved it. Lisa was doing it by the book. She had her outline prepared and the characters, and the day before it was to begin on October 31, she got out her outline and looked at it, and all her characters and emailed me "Ready! Set! Go!" And asked me if I had looked at the book she had given me.

I didn't answer the part of her email where she said "have you read the book I gave you, it has so much helpful information in it."

And then to my own huge surprise I did not wait till day after election or two days after that. The election was on Tuesday of course, and on Sunday I sat down to try to write my novel. I got exactly nowhere. I described what the weather was out my window and what my yard looked like, and hoped something would come into my mind to write about, but nothing came into my mind.

"That's OK" I said to myself, "at least you broke the ice with writing again." I hadn't written in 2 months, it was good to break the ice. And I clicked on my news forum and talked about the election with everyone. And then went back to reading *Sense and Sensibility.*

And the next morning, I guess it was Monday, I clicked on my machine to go back to writing my novel. And again I described the weather and my yard, but this time it worked, a story came. I decided to write about Ruthie's new love affair. And whether it was because I was reading *Sense and Sensibility,* which is about the love affairs of both of the two sisters, or because it is something that everyone knows, I thought "what a perfect topic for a novel, my friend's love affair, this is the classic novel topic." And I got totally excited. I was going to write a novel and it was going to be about Ruthie's new love affair. And so I wrote about Ruthie's whole life, and this was great, I actually had a chapter, Chapter 1.

And I said to myself "I am writing a novel, and it is called *Ruthie Has a New Love*" and I was so happy. And the next day in the pool I told everyone about it and suggested they write a novel too, after all it was just the beginning of the month.

But for some reason Chapter 2 did not take off where I left off. There was no long flow of narrative. The first chapter had been the whole background to the love affair, the second chapter was the love affair. And I don't know why that one didn't work. It was very short and I didn't have very much to say. I realize now that was the morning of the election. I guess I forgot all about the election when I sat down to write my second chapter about her new love affair and wasn't able to get it off the ground.

Then we voted and went swimming. And I came home and read *Sense and Sensibility*.

And then it was the 3rd morning. And there was just no way I could sit at my computer and not write about the election. I knew I was taking my novel off course, but what else could I do. I had a lot of feelings about the election, because on the local level I had lost big time. I hadn't gotten what I wanted and I got what I didn't want. But by the time I finished that chapter I was at peace with myself about it all, it helped me.

And the next morning I just wrote about my own life again, I wrote about my yesterday. Since all my short stories had been about my own life, about my yesterday, when I emailed Lisa (she had been emailing me every day to give me pep talk about my novel) I said "I started it, it was going great guns, I was writing about my friend's love affair, but I got off course, and now I am just writing about my yesterday."

And she emailed back "you always write about your yesterday, here is your chance to write a novel, do it!" She was completely dismayed that I had gone back to writing what I always write. And she told me about their word count and I should go register at the site, and no one is allowed to talk about what they are writing, or to show their writing to anyone on the site, they can only say their word count. And she told me about her word count and her plot and her characters, and asked "did you read that book I gave you, it will help you."

And I went over and registered at the site. They asked for a screen name, so I chose Desert Broom. Altho Lisa thinks it is desert bloom, which is a nice name too. And because I had registered there, I got the first week pep talk letter they sent out to everyone, which I didn't read but I was very glad to get it. I liked being part of this thing and it really made me feel part of it that I got it.

On the 4th day I knew I was off course and would never get back on course. Unless Ruthie called me again with an update about her love affair, there was nothing I could say about it at all. And so I just cracked jokes about my novel. I said "my novel has a first chapter about Ruthie's new love affair, and at the end of the month she will call with an update, so it will have a last chapter about it, and then there will be nothing in-between, I will write about my yesterday for the whole novel."

But then to my surprise Ruthie called that evening.

"O Anne so much is happening it could be a book," she said.

"A novel" I said.

Altho I sure wasn't going to tell Ruthie I was writing a novel about everything she told me on the phone. And she told me all about the developments in her new love affair, and all the new surprise developments with her boyfriend in college who she had never gotten over, they are now on email together. And when she talked about him, she said "this is all such a secret, what he confided to me in email, you must promise not to tell anyone, not even Bill." And I promised. But when she opened up the conversation "there are so many new developments, this could be a book," my first thought was "O good! now I have a new chapter for my novel." And I listened intently to everything she said.

And the next day it all went into my novel. "Ruthie will murder me" I thought "if she ever finds out, but Lisa will be so pleased I introduced new characters." The college boyfriend who I was not to breathe a word about, was the new character in my novel. And that evening Ruthie and I had tête-à-tête with our Higher Selves on the phone about both these relationships and what they mean in Ruthie's life now, and what Ruthie is supposed to be doing. And so I had another chapter, I said everything her Higher Self said about Ruthie and the two men.

I thought "Goody! it is a real novel again."

But there were no more phone calls after that. And so it was back to writing my yesterday and of course there was a huge drama about buying new computer for Bill, that was a major event in my life. I wrote up the whole experience of being in Office Depot. It was such a big experience for me, buying this computer and monitor and printer, that the next day I wrote it all up. And the day after that I could not even write. I tried to force myself to do it, and one sentence eked out. And I shut down the machine and went in to read. I had exhausted myself buying the new computer and then writing it up the next day.

We must have bought the computer on a Friday. Saturday I wrote it up. And Sunday I could not write one word. I took a day off, it was my first day off in writing my novel. It was the climax of the Full Moon too I remember, that beautiful Full Moon. Alas for me all that full moon energy went into the new computer. If my novel has any climax point that is it, and it is about going shopping. Such is my life, but I don't know if a novel it makes.

And then I went back to my daily life in a far more low-keyed way. Just short dreamy chapters about my morning and my yesterday. The teeny uneventful things which pass thru a day. Listening to an old friend's message on my answering machine, feeding the cat. But I liked doing it. I liked waking up each morning and writing new chapter for my novel. It was such a pleasant way to start a day. It seemed so much easier than trying to write a brand new short story each morning when I woke up, because a story has to have so much life in it to stand on its own.

And now that *Sense and Sensibility* was over, and I was going to see if I could enjoy the other books at the bottom of the pile, I realized I just wanted something to read. And I thought "maybe that is all a chapter has to do, give someone something to read." It is like writing without a pressure, no pressure to deliver. All you want to do is give someone something so they can keep reading, and things could be as easy as pie for me. Maybe it is a lazy man's solution to writing. But after all these years of trying to deliver something in a story, I liked just meandering down my life, and writing down whatever comes. It is like drifting down a big river. I might have my line out, but some of the time no fish bites. But I am still enjoying the ride. I love it, in fact. And that is the whole truth. I love writing a novel and I don't know why. Just that it is relaxing and fun and easy and enjoyable.

And I found out from Lisa's email the novel has to be 50,000 words, 170 pages, and we end on November 30th. And I was now getting regular pep talks from them, which I was not reading, but I was glad to be getting. And one of the pep talks I did read a little of and I liked. He said "this is just to serve you, to get you writing, and however it serves you, it is doing what it is supposed to be doing." And Lisa was still telling me about her plot and her characters and how she has to make a graph on her hard drive to keep track of all of them, and am I doing that too? But she has fallen behind in word count and has to rush to keep up.

And I wrote back "we are both doing fine in our novels and that is great" and "O Lisa I thank you from the bottom of my heart for getting me into this, I love it."

And Lisa said she had registered her word count on the site. And the other morning, after I wrote a totally loopy chapter-- never have I been more at odds and ends with myself and that chapter shows it; every instinct I have says "take it out," but I will leave it in, maybe novels need a loopy chapter-- I did the word count on everything I had written and entered it on the site.

And they make you post it all to prove it is that many words. I had found out from Lisa that for November we are not supposed to edit. We are only supposed "to write like the wind" according to Lisa. And after November 30th we are given one month to edit what we have written.

So I took the whole mish-mosh of what I had written, 9/10ths with uncorrected typos, and posted it. They said "our robot counter will just count the words to verify your word count and then delete it." Which is what happened. And it turned out I have 47,000 words, which is very close to what they want. In fact with that loopy chapter which I wasn't sure if I was going to include, it would have put me over. And then they had me write the name of my novel. And instead of calling it "Ruthie Has A New Love," I decided to call it "Daddy-o," which means something to me personally but doesn't mean anything to anyone else. But I thought "no one pays attention to the meaning of novels' names anyway." And they wanted a description of my novel, so I wrote a description. And they wanted an extract, so I put in an extract from my first chapter about Ruthie because that is the only one which reads like a novel.

And then I wanted picture for my book cover. And I tried to upload the drawing Layla had done of the belly dancer dancing, but I couldn't get it to upload. And then I emailed Lisa "what is your name there so I can put you on my buddy list?" And I told her my word count is 47,000 because I like to blab a lot when I write.

And because Lisa was at work last evening with nothing to do, she went over and looked at everything about my novel. She saw my verified word count and guess what? To my utter surprise and amazement, Lisa is impressed with me. I don't think anyone has ever been impressed with me or proud of me in my whole life. It is such a totally new feeling. I am stunned. She said "you might be the winner!" I had no idea this thing was about winning, that there is anything to win. And she said I have more words than the founder. That is what really impressed Lisa, that the founder of National Write a Novel in a Month, the man who wrote that book on how to do it, I have more words than he does. Maybe it is silly to be happy that Lisa is impressed with me and proud of me just for a lot of words. But I've never had this experience before. Nothing I wrote has ever been published. Even Lisa who has read every single one of my short stories on email for past 3 years, has never been proud of me or impressed with me till I had a lot of words. I am going to email my mother that I have a lot of words, so she can be proud of me and impressed with me too. Altho I will send Lisa's email along with it, to give her the hint that she is supposed to be proud and impressed by this. She might not know that, only Lisa knows that because she is on this site. And Lisa said her novel ground to a halt because so many other things in her life came up. Lisa works at a TV station, plus she teaches art, she has classes. She said she will try again another time.

And I sent her the drawing of the belly dancer Layla did, on email. And I sent her my password and screen name there, and because Lisa was at work with nothing to do, she turned it into a book cover and posted it under my screen name. Along with my description of novel, extract from novel, and WORD COUNT!! It wasn't exactly what I had in mind. That drawing by Layla is so expressive and feelingful, and dreamy, when Lisa put in Daddy-o in huge big block letters it overwhelmed the drawing, it lost its feeling. I said "let's change to one of your watercolors of the desert mountains." But Lisa said "I like the dancer." She has my name on it as Desert Bloom, instead of desert broom which is a weed in my backyard. But maybe I should go with that name instead. Altho maybe I will switch to Palo Verde. I think I would rather be Ms. Verde than Ms. Broom, and the palo verde is the tree out my window, it grows all over the desert wild.

Lisa emailed back "don't think about your cover now, go back to writing like the wind." She is concerned I won't make the 50,000 and make it over the top. She wants me to be a winner. LOL she is my coach.

And it is very nice to have a coach. I don't know which I have enjoyed more in writing my novel, writing my novel or having Lisa as my coach. She's a wonderful coach. Even tho she was so disappointed in me at first, I now surpassed her wildest dreams because I have more words than the founder.

November 26

How I met Bill at the Paradox

It rained in the night. The air coming in my open window is all fresh smelling. And fresh from rain-on-desert-smelling. Cold fresh air, but nice! Rain is such a treat when you have not had it for a long time.

I didn't know it had rained in night. I looked out my open window when I woke up and thought "for sure today it is going to rain." It was all misty out, and the sky is full of thick misty rain clouds. But I saw my patio was wet, and so it had already rained.

I had harmonious dreams last night, and harmonious dreams when I fell asleep in middle of evening while watching TV. In the nap dream we were all marching somewhere together, and everyone was having fun and kidding around. And so was I. I went from person to person, kidding and laughing and making jokes, being friendly.

When I woke up from that nap dream, just a minute before Bill returned from the movies, I was in awe. Imagine a dream where everyone gets along and has fun with everyone! Imagine a dream where I get along with everyone and have fun with everyone! Hahaha I guess the New Age has begun. I guess the new world is here.

The dream I had before I awoke wasn't as vivant as that one, as exuberant and outgoing. I just remembered I found 3 new green blouses in a pile. It is my favorite blouse, and I like that apple green color. In real life I do own 3 blouses like that, but because they were my favorite blouse, I wore them all the time, so they are totally stained now. In my dream there were 3 fresh new ones and I was so happy, just what I wanted! So it was a quiet dream of satisfaction.

Bill just woke up and said "Hi Bean, even tho it is raining out, we are going to go out." And he is in the kitchen heating up his cup of coffee. I wonder if I will see them arrive thru my open window. If he will go to that chair I can see out my window, or that table too far to my right to be able to see.

A little sparrow is on my tree chirping at me. Two sparrows now! They flew off! Now they arrived back again! They love this weather, it makes them feel so alive. O it is so nice to breathe in this rain-on-desert scented air. It's such a different scent to the air. It is scented with the earth.

O sparrow is back! Facing the other way, I can see his back. It looks like bark of tree, those kind of stripes or strata. O Bill and Bean are out at the table, I can't see them unless I stretch and look out. "Hello little buddy" he said to Beanie when he arrived at table, "you like this weather."

Jan's email yesterday said "the hum of the dishwasher is on and now I am going to put up the laundry, not very exciting life." And I thought "me too, I have the same life."

Bill just said "I will keep the dog outside, because kitty is in the house, she is in my room on the bed." I guess kitty slept with Bill again, and she hasn't woken up yet. I am glad she was not in the rain last night, but instead curled up with Bill in his soft warm bed. O now he is asking Bean if he wants to go to Wales. Because Beanie is part Corgi, and the Corgis come from Wales, in Bill's mind Beanie is always dreaming of Wales. The first thing Bill said when he woke up was "Beanie will like this weather, this is how it is in Wales."

The cigarettes I ordered on internet did not arrive. After the pool yesterday we went to discount cigarette store in the shopping center of our supermarket, and I bought a carton there. The day before I had bought 4 packs from him because I thought the cigarettes could arrive any day. But when I woke up yesterday, I thought "I have no idea when they will arrive, I will buy carton and feel secure."

Bill had told me the man who owned that discount smokes store was Italian, "he has an accent but you can understand him." So when I went in and heard his thick accent I said "are you Italian?" And he said "no." There were two college students in there buying Sherman cigarettes. And I got excited and said "Shermans! they were right around the corner from me when I lived in New York." It does seem to me Sherman cigarettes come from Union Square in Manhattan.

I remember when I first saw people smoking them, two hippies in the Paradox macrobiotic restaurant in my neighborhood in the Sixties. I wasn't a cigarette smoker then, but when they offered me one I tried it. They said "it is Sherman's, it is all natural." It was a long thin cigarette in a lavender wrapper, instead of white. And were maybe flat in a box, instead of in a pack.

The 2 college students ignored me and acted as if I had not spoken. And when the man behind the counter asked what I wanted, I heard his thick accent and said "are you Italian?" And he said "no" and then waited for me to say what kind of cigarettes I wanted. I thought "it isn't my day, no one wants to talk to me," so I said "which are your cheapest cigarettes?" And he named a brand. I said "I never heard of that, how much is Liggetts?" He said their price, and I said "that is only 25 cents more a pack and I know Liggetts and I like them, so I will get 4 packs of Liggetts."

I thought he wasn't going to talk to me either, but to my surprise when he was ringing up my order he said "are you from New York?"

I said "yes."

He said "where?"

I said "I was born on Riverside Drive."

He said "I know Riverside Drive, I lived on Broadway and 83rd Street."

"Broadway and 83rd Street!" I said, "I know that, you take the IRT and get off on 86th Street."

He said "yes."

He said he went to Columbia.

I said "I went to CCNY," and he smiled, he knew CCNY.

So when I went in yesterday to buy a carton, I said "hello new york," when I walked in. And told him I had lived at 85th and Riverside for a few years, "we got off at the same subway stop" I told him, "the IRT stop on Broadway." I realized it was the first time since I have been in Tucson I have said "IRT" to anyone. It was all there on my tongue and in my mind, it popped out so easily. But afterwards it felt like past life bleeding thru. Once my life was the IRT and now it's not. But of course I do know his subway station very well. Not only because I did live briefly at 85th and Riverside, but because it was the subway station I got off to see my shrink, she lived one block up, and I went to my shrink for a long time when I was very young.

I still remember that hippie couple who offered me a Shermans at the Paradox. I did start to smoke soon after that and as a result the first cigarettes I bought were Shermans. I bought them at Gem Spa, a candy and cigar store on St Marks Place and 2nd Avenue. You could get them in dark brown paper covered cigarettes and maybe violet too.

I only started smoking cigarettes because I was a pot smoker then, and wanted something I could smoke in public, and Shermans seemed a solution. I liked to smoke and they looked more like a pot cigarette than a regular cigarette. In fact at first I hoped people would realize I was smoking a regular cigarette and not a pot one.

Altho I must have quickly advanced to regular cigarettes, because when I met Bill at the Paradox the following summer, I was smoking Kents. I chose Kents because that is what my shrink smoked. And I bought them in the bodega next door to the Paradox.

Bill was working at the Paradox then when I first met him. And when we discovered we were both cig smokers, if we didn't have any, we would ask the other for a cig. And one afternoon I arrived and said "do you have a cig?" And he said "no, I was just going to ask you," and I said "I will go next door and buy a pack." I knew he smoked Winstons, and I smoked Kents, and I went and bought his brand Winstons, and handed it to him. And even tho these were all my own decisions, to buy his brand, to hand it to him, as soon as I did, I thought "Just like a guy! That's what guys do! they are selfish and they take advantage of you! they don't care about girls at all!"

And I got a cup of tea, they had free bancha tea next to cash register, and sat down at the long table in middle, and thought about what I would order. And when I looked up, there was Bill standing by me. He had gone next door to the bodega and bought a pack of Kents, my brand, and handed it to me. And I was so floored at this kindness and generosity and consideration, he had gone out and bought my brand for me, that I married him. Not right away of course, but it is how he won my heart. I trusted him.

I don't remember now who first took me to the Paradox. Even tho it was right around the corner from me, someone had to take me, I didn't know about it. Someone who knew about it took me, some guy I was friends with at the time, but I don't remember now who? After that I must have gone on my own, because when I sat at the table with the two hippies who offered me their Sherman cigarettes I was by myself. Maybe that was the first time I had gone by myself. It seems to me I felt like quite a stranger there, and I was grateful for their friendliness to me.

It was a hang-out, and eventually I came all the time, and spent all my time there. But at first I just came for a meal. I liked it because ordinary rules did not apply. There was one very long table in the middle, people sat around it and ate. And the Paradox had a lot of cats, and the cats would walk up and down the table as people ate, and if they didn't finish their plate, they would push it over for the cat to eat. I seem to remember a gray cat with 6 toes. And I was a cat owner then and I loved cats, I loved being in a restaurant where cats were allowed.

Another thing about rules didn't apply, is if someone didn't finish their meal and left it there, someone else would sit down and eat it. I remember once ordering shrimp there, they made it delicious, but for some reason as soon as I started to eat it I noticed I wasn't hungry, so I said "anyone want this?" and 8 people did, and I handed the bowl to one of them.

O there is Bill's kitty Priscilla. She is sitting by the tree. I guess she woke up and got out of Bill's bed. She is looking up. I guess she hopes a bird will land there.

Now she is looking up at me, our eyes meeting. She does look like a miniature bob cat, Bill is right. O she sure is pretty! All those multi colors and patterns, and with so much yellow. God she is a beauty. And she has her winter coat, all furry and lush, and she is not skinny anymore. Bill feeds her 5 times a day. O she is looking at me with tiger eyes. She turned around and walked off with black fluffy tail.

I was a school teacher then and went to the Paradox in the evenings. I had supper and hung out and then went home. When Abbie and I went to Jamaica for 3 days during Christmas vacation, she was school teacher too then, I came back with a tan and told everyone at the Paradox I had been to Jamaica. I didn't have friends there yet, I just sat at the big table and told it to the big table at large.

It wasn't till summer vacation and I was off and would arrive when the Paradox opened at noon and spend afternoon there, and come back in the evening, that I began to make friends there.

Mike befriended me, he was the first. He gave me a cookie; the Paradox used to make these big cookies with raisins. I thought he was a boy who wanted to ask me out. How come he was being nice to me and giving me a cookie? But he didn't seem to ask me out, he just seemed to want to be friends with me. I didn't know about being gay then. I didn't realize he was interested in me as a friend.

His other friend was Angela. She was an older woman, a very rich woman from 5th Avenue, who had house in the Hamptons. This was Mike's other friend. Maybe Mike worked at the Paradox too then. And so Angela and Mike and I all sat together at the big table in middle when it was cold out, and when the weather turned warm, at big communal table in backyard.

I was too shy to talk to Angela myself, I wasn't used to grown-ups, I was shy with them, but she and Mike were best friends. Until she hired Mike to bartend one of her parties at her fancy apartment. I think Mike wasn't used to being treated like a servant, his feelings got hurt. But before that they used to make each other laugh and totally enjoyed each others company. I never opened up my mouth when Mike and Angela were talking, I was shy with Angela. But Mike knew everyone there, it was how I got to meet the people at the Paradox, those who ate there and those who worked there, Mike made me feel at home there, that was very nice of him.

One evening I arrived, it was summer, so I was sitting in the outside yard, and to my surprise one of the young hippies who had arrived, or young women, turned out to be my cousin Goldi from Tucson. I guess the Paradox was on a circuit if my Tucson cousin knew about it and arrived there. We were happy and surprised to recognize each other, but she was in one world I was in another then, we were both so young and on our way.

I am sure I introduced her to Mike, but I bet she has no idea that was the same Mike, that 10 or 15 years later, when she decided to live in New York City and was staying with my aunt Esther. And I said "my friend Mike has a loft, he may be looking for a roommate." And she did become his roommate and they became very close friends. And that was an odd time for me, because I wanted to be close friends with her too and she seemed to have no use for me. And Mike had stopped being close friends with me, and I couldn't get him back. But he and Goldi were very very close.

Now I am not mad about it, altho at the time I had feelings about it, a lot of feelings. But now it just seems all constellations move in their own way and best thing is to just let them. The constellation of Goldi and the constellation of Mike joined and were so close, and I was left out, not included. But now it seems so what? It has nothing to do with me.

It may have been toward the end of July and I was sitting on the Paradox stoop waiting for it to open. I forget now what time it opened, maybe 11 am. And a small skinny guy with an airplane bag sat down on the stoop next to me waiting for it to open too. And we fell into conversation. He was very easy to talk to, and we got along swimmingly.

And that evening when I returned for supper and was sitting at the big communal table in the middle of the restaurant eating my meal, and there was a long line for take-out I guess, and the line was right behind my back, I turned around and noticed the small flight bag the young guy had this morning.

There was a very cute guy in line and he had that flight bag. And so I said "I know that flight bag!" And maybe I tried to say "doesn't it belong to someone else?" or whatever. Whatever I did say, the young man refused to answer me, he just stayed on line for his take-out food. And I thought to myself, "the guys I am attracted to never like me back." And of course that turned out to be Bill. The young guy I had talked to in the morning was his friend James from San Diego, they were both in New York City together and both staying at an apartment of a friend of James.

Just as James had so easily fallen into good fellowship with me, been so easy for me to talk to, and so appreciative and so responsive, and fun-- we talked about movie stars together and French movie stars and Jean Luc Godard and

Godard's wife who was a movie star then, all the topics I liked to talk about, but didn't think boys liked to talk about at all. Apparently James had made friends with everyone in rock bands and those who managed rock bands and one of them was a rock band producer or manager, and James had gotten him to let him stay at his apartment, a fancier apartment in a fancier neighborhood. And when Bill had arrived in NYC from San Diego, Bill was staying there too. That is why it was the same flight bag, James had sent him to the Paradox to get take-out food for him. He was going to put the take-out food in the flight bag.

"How come you didn't talk to me when I talked to you on line?" I asked Bill later.

"Because I thought you were a bitch and were talking to me to be a bitch and put me down."

It's amazing boys and girls ever do get together, we are all so suspicious of each other, and suspect each other of worst intentions. He thought I was friendly to him just to be mean to him, and I thought he was just using me to get a free pack of cigarettes, but in fact we liked each other.

It must have been the same day or the day after he bought me the pack of Kents, that I arrived and he was sitting at the table reading a *Scientific America,* and I sat down next to him. And maybe it was picture of the Earth going in an elliptic around the Sun. I remember it was something I was very interested to figure out when I was in an advanced science class in high school. I had friend then, Irving, who was a top student, and he helped me figure out how it worked out, the elliptic, but I had forgotten, and I sat with Bill and tried to figure it out again.

And I was so relaxed and happy and comfortable to be sitting next to Bill as he smoked his Winstons and I smoked my Kents, looking at the *Scientific America* together and trying to figure out the elliptic of the Earth around the Sun, talking about science together, which always interested me. And feeling like Bill was a friend, as comfortable and happy with him as I had been with Irving Feldman all those years ago.

And that was the start of me and Bill being boyfriend and girlfriend .... everything else happened quickly after that. First we went thru the ups and downs of beginning relationships. You get together, you break up, you get together again. Then in the winter we began living together. And of course there were ups and downs.

But when push comes to shove, the '60s ended, the Paradox ended, my friendship with Mike ended, even New

York City ended, and where we are is the sun came out after the rain, Bill's kitty is off having an adventure, Bill is in front yard with Beanie. And I think I might take a little sun in the backyard garden couch, if the red cover on it is not too wet from the rain.

And Caren's brother Jack, from next door, just knocked on the door to say "I brought you and Bill chocolate cake for Thanksgiving present and the newspaper for Bill so he can read the sports."

And I said "you are an angel, Jack." And he flapped his arms and said "I don't know where my wings are..."

The end, Tucson Arizona, November 26, 2008

by the author on June 12, 2009

I hope you enjoyed reading my novel.

Haiku Helen and I published this book together. She did the cover drawings (back and front) and designed the cover. Neither of us has any experience in book publishing, please forgive us for all mistakes we have made.

Since I have several other books already written, we plan to publish those next.

What Happened Next recounts events in my life after *Ruthie Has a New Love* takes place.

Girl Blog from Tucson and ***More Girl Blog from Tucson*** are the stories I wrote about my life in Tucson and in NYC before I wrote *Ruthie Has a New Love.*

Love, Anne

Here are chapters from 2 of these books soon to be published by us (Haiku Helen Press).

A chapter from

What Happened Next

January 9, 2009

Car mirror falls off

Well I guess today marks the day of the season which no one talks about (because it doesn't have a name) but I call it "waiting for Spring" and it is one of my favorite seasons. It seems to start the day after you think "OK I've had it with winter! I am now ready for spring." And it's like "at your service, madam" the next day "waiting for Spring begins".

I don't know if the sap has actually moved up the trees in my yard, if the tops of the trees are actually reaching for heaven, which is the exact beginning of "waiting for spring," but my eyes are drawn to the tops of the trees looking for it. And maybe that is enough. The field of activity will take place there and I am already in position watching. Hahaha like already taking your seat at a sporting event, you know the game will begin any minute.

And last night the Moon sure looked Full, especially by the wee hours of the morning. I bet instant Moon hits exact Full "waiting for spring" will begin. At the very least it is in the mind's eye now. And Buddhist New Year (maybe on the next full moon or new moon) is coming up.

Well all our outdoor kitties seem to have discovered Priscilla has soft berth here. They know food is always put out for her. And we have been having lots of visitors during the night when we sleep. Priscilla sleeps with Bill of course, and she sleeps to noon. Bill's friend Jim wasn't surprised to hear it. He said his cat sleeps with him too but she sprawls in the middle of the bed, he gets pushed to the edge and finally it is so uncomfortable he moves over to the sofa. So then she gets up to sleep with him there.

O my goodness! a cat is screeching in heat! I bet it is our Priscilla! She is totally embarrassing herself. O now she is spitting and fighting! I can't see it, I can hear it. She does not treat her boyfriends well, she spits and fights and bites. It makes Beanie seem so good by contrast, all he does is walk quietly around his yard and bury his cookies. He has nothing to do with this absolutely wild cat party going on. It's like watching one child in second grade classroom sitting calmly at his desk with his hands folded waiting for his homework assignment while all the rest are hanging from the chandeliers and doing spitballs.

Yesterday when we arrived at Jerry's pool for our swim in the 2nd hand Chrysler (truck is still in the shop) Bill got out, but I had to organize all my stuff, put my purse in my swim bag, find my towel, take off my long sleeve shirt etc. Maybe it was when I was taking off my long sleeve shirt, I merely bumped something, not hard, and I felt something fall and when I turned around to find out, it was the mirror attached to the windshield. I knew Bill would take that very seriously and I called him back.

"O NO!" he said, "it's your fault, you have too much stuff."

It looked like it had just been glued up on there, so I said "wait! I'll get Jerry! he has all the tools."

I thought we could just glue it back. Jerry came out with me, but he said the same thing happened to him last week, he told Bill he went to Pep Boys and bought the kit, but it takes 24 hours to dry, and he learned the hard way he should have made an x with a pencil to mark the spot. Bill said it happened to him years back and there is a place on Columbus Road which did it in 10 minutes. Jerry said he didn't know about that.

So Bill said "Get back in the car Anne, we'll go over there now."

He was worried the place wouldn't be there any more, "things change" he kept saying "and not always for the best." And we went there and it wasn't there. So we tried Columbus Glass and Mirror, the place Jerry had guessed Bill meant, but they don't do cars. So we went to Pep Boys and he said we have to go to an auto body and glass shop, and gave us a card for one by Swapmeet.

Bill said "I'm not going all the way over there."

So he said "well then go home and look up one in the phone book."

So we got home, and Bill said "Look on the computer and find one close to us."

They were all far away, but one had a close-to-us address so I called. I don't know why the guy, he said his name is Cort, found it all so humorous, but whatever I said he cracked a joke, which naturally put me in a good mood, it made it all seem so no-big-deal. Car terminology is just not at my fingertips. I should have said "the mirror fell off the windshield," but the word windshield was not in my mind, so instead I told him the story.

"I just bumped it the least little bit and it fell off" I said. I thought I was clear. But it was a Tucson auto glass company, he kept trying to understand what glass was broken. Clearly he thought I was an idiot. So he approached the problem with baby steps to try to figure out what was broken.

"What kind of car do you have?" he asked, and I told him all about our 2nd hand Chrysler, I did not understand why he wanted that info. But finally it dawned on him what the problem was.

"The mirror fell off your windshield?" he asked.

"YES!" I said "YES!"

"So no glass is broken?"

"No, no glass is broken."

"Is the mirror broken?"

"No" I said, "it fell into my lap, so it had a soft ride home" and I burst out laughing.

"Well that's no problem" he said, "this happens all the time, it just happened to me this morning because I have a very old car, the UV in the sunlight simply eats up the adhesive, it happens in new cars too. It wasn't your fault it happened, it would have happened anyway." I had told him I bumped it and Bill said it was my fault for having too much stuff.

I guess he doesn't have a shop because he said he will come over to fix it.

I said "you will want to be paid in cash not with check or the card."

He said "right."

I said "how much will it cost, I'll look all over and see how much cash I have."

"15 dollars" he said.

"15 dollars!" I said "that is great! that is nothing."

And then he made another joke "did I say $15 I meant $150." I knew it was a joke.

And he said "that is a joke."

"I knew it" I said.

"When do you want me to come over?"

"Now" I said.

"Now?" he said.

"Yes, now." Bill had said he wanted it fixed now.

“OK” he said, “I'm coming over, what is your address?” And I sure thanked him a lot and got off the phone to tell Bill the good news. Bill said he has a $20 and a ten. I said "good! give him the $20, 5 dollars for tip."

And then I went to the couch in backyard to relax in sunshine, the house is ice cold. My Higher Self said he will be there in 15 minutes so I just lay there and chit-chatted with my Higher Self and communicated with Cort in my mind too. And Beanie came out so he could lounge next to me on the ground and have gazillion pets. And eventually I heard what sounded like voices in my front yard but I could not be sure. And then Bill came out and said "it's done, but we have to wait 10 minutes, then I will take you to Edith Ball Pool and we will go to Sunflower to buy food for Beanie and groceries."

"Great!" I said "great!"

"Did you give him the $20" I asked.

"Yes" he said, "he was very appreciative."

"Good!" I said "good!"

And 15 minutes later we set off for the swimming pool again, a different pool tho cause Jerry's is closed. And it was a really nice swim and Jeff was there, I was surprised and happy to see him. And delicious hot showers. Jerry's showers have not gotten warmer, they have gotten colder. Now all the girls are happy when it turns tepid from ice cold, the day we thought it would be hot are just a memory.

And we did nice little shopping at Sunflower. Bill waited in car. There were a lot of instructions.

"Don't touch the mirror!" he told me, "don't slam the

door! and have all your stuff organized so you don't bump it!"

"I promise I will be very careful" I said.

When we got out of Sunflower I guess sunset was starting. I really rarely do get to see sunsets, none of my windows face it, and usually I am watching tv anyway. But when things go wrong, hahaha, somehow it always means you are driving in the car at sunset, you do get to see the sunsets. Of course usually it is a beauty show involving pink. But yesterday was one of my favorites because you so rarely see it. It all involved yellow light, a pale yellow, almost lemony. It was so subtle and so beautiful it took my breath away. I loved it. And all's well that ends well.

Girl Blog from Tucson

My life in NYC and Tucson

Chapter 1

How it all started

I had dropped out of college when I was 20, and I went to look for a job. I went to The American Museum of Natural History and called on the house telephone to Lew. My friend from college, Pam, had worked for him on a fellowship from NSF. And she had brought him home for dinner. He seemed like a nice man, but I had been too shy to notice. I was intimidated a grown up was in the house, but he was nice for a grown up. I called him on the house telephone and said "Dr. Irizarri, I am Anne, Pam Holder's friend, you had dinner at our house, I am looking for a job."

And he said "stay right there, Anne, I am coming down, you are an answer to a prayer." And he came down and told me he was just wishing he had 25 extra hours a week to do the things he wanted, and since he didn't have them, he wanted a Girl Friday to do them for him, and he had no idea about how to go about finding a Girl Friday, and he hired me on the spot.

Then I called my mother. "I decided to drop out of college for one semester" I told her.

"But what will you do" she said.

"I will get a job" I said.

"But who will ever hire you" she said.

"Dr. Lewis Irizarri, anthropologist at The American Museum of Natural History just did" I told her.

That was a wonderful job and Lew turned out to be the loveliest employer I ever had as well as a great friend who has lasted me my whole life.

Lew made a lot of things possible for me. Above all he gave employment to me any time I needed a job, which made possible the changes I was making in my life.

It caused a huge commotion at home when I decided to drop out of college, even tho I told them it was just for one semester. When my mother said "what will you do" it shut her right up that I said Lew had hired me. After all I was working at the American Museum of Natural History for an anthropologist, a curator of ethnology. Their whole idea of college was so it would give me a job. And the job I had for Lew sounded good on paper. Or should I say, where I was working and who I was working for, sounded very good on paper. They had no idea what my actual job was. They probably thought I was a research assistant.

"Annie dropped out of college" my dad told his sisters.

"O no!" they said, "what will she do."

"She is working for an anthropologist at the American Museum of Natural History, she is his research assistant."

"O that doesn't sound too bad" they said.

It sounded like a job I would get when I had gotten my degree, before I became a school teacher like everyone else in the family.

I was living at home then. And I would get dressed each day and take the bus and 3 subway trains to the Museum. My job was 5 hours a day. I would arrive at the Museum and Lew would make a list of what he wanted. And I would set out to do it. A friend of Lew's and mine at the Museum, a nice girl from Wisconsin, used to refer to my job as "are you still doing Lew's shopping for him?" Which was an accurate description of my job, altho Lew and I both preferred calling it, I was his Girl Friday.

My first assignment was to go to Madison Square Gardens and get their schedule of their college basketball games. I was told to make sure it is the college games. Then he sent me to the 42nd Street Library to look up zip codes of some people he was writing to in Maine. It was all on a list. So I went from one place to another. I realize now everything Lew had me get for him or look up for him, people no longer hire a Girl Friday to do that for them, it is all on internet.

But I went to Madison Square Garden and got him the schedule of the college basketball games, I went to the ticket office. Then I walked over to the 42nd Street Library and looked up all the things he wanted me to look up. And then I walked along 5th Avenue and window shopped, and I think I bought myself a pair of shoes. And he wanted a large box of Kleenex and I bought that for him. And in all my long time of working for him, it was the only error I ever made. It turns out when Lew had written Kleenex down on the paper he meant Kleenex. I had bought tissues. Kleenex pops up. I had to exchange it.

Then because he was a member of the faculty at Columbia University, or something, he had library privileges there. He was allowed to take out books. And he had a long list of books he wanted. That was the only assignment which was a little hard, carrying all those books back to the Museum. I guess I took the bus, but still I had to walk to the bus stop with them and then walk to the Museum.

All my jobs were variations on the above it seems to me. I kept track of my own hours, and Lew paid me 50 dollars a week for 25 hours. I felt like I got the best of the bargain because I would do long window shopping and shopping on way back to the Museum. And I was astounded years later, when Lew had had a slew of Girl Fridays who followed in my footsteps, when he told Janet, I was the best of all of them. Janet said his newest one is always lying down in the ladies room at the Museum.

Pam and Ellie had worked for Lew on a Fellowship. Ellie and Lew remained best friends, she would visit us in the office. Ellie was my age, so when June came, she graduated Hunter College, and my assignment for that day was to buy all the stuff so we would have party for Ellie in the office. I thought "this sure is a neat job, going to work means buying the candy and cake and having a party with Ellie in the office."

A few months after I began working for Lew, one of my boyfriends, Alan, returned home from Italy, and was staying at his parents' house in Queens. He called me up and said "I have decided to write a novel and I think you would be easy to live with while I write my novel, do you want to share an apartment with me in the East Village?"

I had a big crush on Alan then. I think he had other girlfriends. He said he chose me because "you won't bother me while I am writing." And I accepted the offer even tho it was hardly an expression of passionate love. It had been my dream for long time to live with a guy.

I didn't know what the East Village was, I had never lived there, I had always lived with roommates on the Upper West Side of Manhattan while I had been in college. But Alan picked me up, and we found an apartment on East 12th Street between A and B. So I told my parents, "I am moving into an apartment with Sue Pruitt." She had been my friend from City College and come home one evening for dinner, and my brother and father were smitten with her, such a beautiful blond, and my mom liked her too. I said "Alan is helping me move my stuff," and she said "OK." And I moved in with Alan on East 12th Street.

I completely forgot my parents thought I was living with Sue Pruitt, till one night, when I was in bed with Alan, two young men knocked on the door. I could hear them from the other side of the wall. And one was a friend from college. He said "Anne, your mother gave me your address, and I am here with my friend Steve, to take you and Sue out." I don't think I opened the door. I called thru the wall, "I am not living with Sue, I am living with Alan." And they went away. I had had a crush on him in college and he had never responded, and I thought "wow if you wait long enough he did ask me out." But it was too late, I was living with Alan now. Also I realized how much my mom believed I was living with Sue, if she directed the two young men to my apartment so they could take us out on a date.

My mom decided to visit me at the Museum with her new best friend Nicole from Cairo, Egypt. They were both going for their Masters in Public Health at Columbia together. Lew was very gracious to both the women and I took them around, and showed them everything on the 5th floor where the public is not allowed to go. And I also confided to my mom I am not living with Sue, I am living with Alan and I am very happy. Which caused total apoplexy. She had a fit and her whole visit was ruined.

"Why are you so upset" I kept saying, "I am happy, that is all that matters."

"That is not all that matters" she kept saying.

"If you love him why don't you marry him" she said.

"I don't want to get married, I like living with him."

She was very upset about it.

When I walked with Nicole alone I said "I don't know why she is so upset."

I was now 21. I had moved in with Alan month before my 21st birthday. I liked my life at the time. I loved living with Alan in the East Village (we became close after we began living together; he proposed marriage). I loved the East Village, I loved working for Lew at the Museum. Alan was working for his dad. His dad had an attaché case factory on Broom Street. Alan worked in the office. He had all those beautiful clothes he had bought in Rome. And each morning we had breakfast, and then wore very attractive clothes. I was wearing very pretty nylon stockings then, with nice shoes, nice skirt, nice blouse. Maybe Alan wore a suit, and he had an attaché case of course. And we set off for the subway together. Alan had developed the habit of drinking tea when he was in Rome, so we had tea for breakfast. But my craving for coffee had not left, so after I left Alan I stopped at coffee shop for cup of coffee and donut, and then took subway up to the Museum.

And Alan introduced me to pot. I don't know if I would have smoked it, if I wasn't just starting to live with him, and still had huge crush on him, and wasn't yet comfortable in his company. I was trying to please him. So it was a toss up, my reluctance to "take a drug" or my desire to please him. And my desire to please him won. I took the drug, I was willing to try pot. And almost instantly-- maybe not the first time or the second time when nothing happened, but the third time when I got high-- it was a great love affair. It was a love affair which ended very badly, but for a long time pot was a huge joy in my life

It was my first experience of liberation. I just didn't know I could have that. To be free to be myself. And to actually experience my own mind. I found my own mind thrilling, I loved it. And I loved being free to be myself. It was so much fun to be myself.

Chapter 2

Nancy Cantor

I dreamt about Nancy Cantor all night. She was my first friend after college. I graduated college in August. I had to spend that extra summer studying for the finals I had not taken during finals week in June and doing term papers. It was a wild summer, the "Summer of Love". And I had sublet an apartment for the summer on the corner of St Mark's Place. My friend from college, Francine, roomed with me. I was stoned the whole summer and do not know how I managed to take those finals and write those papers. But by end of summer I did, and I got my degree. And then immediately found a job at The Riverdale Children's Agency.

I had gone down for that job because the year before Wendy had worked there. Sometimes I would meet her in Central Park during her lunch hour, right by the Agency, it was at 79th and Madison Avenue. Because Wendy worked there I thought it would be a nice place to work. So I interviewed and they hired me. The woman in charge, Mrs. Streeter, liked me in the interview and hired me. Olive Streeter, the name comes back to me now.

The weekend before I was going to start work, a friend I had been a camp counselor with 3 summers before, invited me to go swimming in Rye, New York, where his parents had their home and where he was staying for the summer. He picked me up in his car at St Mark's Place and First Avenue, and I must have worn my bikini under my sundress, because I remember taking off my dress in the car to show him my new bikini (it was my first bikini) and he said "will it stay up?"

Ken-- his name was Ken-- Ken Adler. I always felt very close to him because one of the times when he had invited me to his parents' house in Rye so I could swim in the bay there, we had been swimming and he said "Anne I have a cramp in my leg, I can't make it back to shore."

And I said "put your hands on my shoulders, I'll swim under you and swim you back to shore," which I did.

At dinner that night he told his parents, "Anne saved me, she rescued me in the water."

And they said "O really" and the conversation moved on. For all the huge drama which goes on in learning how to be a junior life saver when I was 11 years old, all the huge dramatic rescues I did when we took turns playing the victim, the one actual rescue I did was the quietest simplest thing which ever happened. I swam him to shore, he said "thank you," he told his parents at dinner, and it was clear nobody believed us, and that was that.

On my previous visits I had stayed in his big sister's room and it was a beautiful room. Their whole house was a mansion, which made visiting there so much fun for me. I loved swimming in the bay, I liked Ken Adler a lot, and I found it a lot of fun to stay in a mansion, and in the bedroom of this princess sister, it was a bedroom for a princess.

This was the last time I visited there. And on my last day the Princess herself arrived. I finally got to meet her, Margie Adler. And when Ken drove me back to the city, Margie was in the car with us. And when I mentioned I start work the next day at Riverdale Children's Agency, Margie turned to her brother and said "Isn't that where Nancy Cantor works?" Apparently a friend of Margie's named Nancy Cantor worked there and I got so excited.

I was thrilled with the fairy tale princess Margie. I barely knew her, just that car ride back to the city, but I had stayed in her princess bedroom 3 times. In my mind she was Princess Charming. So naturally I saw Nancy Cantor as an extension of her, it was the next best thing to being friends with Margie.

When I arrived the first morning I asked the girl at reception where you check in, "is Nancy Cantor here?" And she said "Nancy is on vacation, she will be back in a week." And I waited the whole week, and then sat by reception when the week was over, to wait for Nancy. Each woman who arrived, I thought "is that Nancy?" Finally one woman arrived and the woman at reception said "that is Nancy Cantor."

So I followed her up the steps, and said, "I am a friend of Margie Adler's, she told me you work here."

Nancy said "I just got back from Nantucket, I rode my bicycle everywhere, I am lost without my bicycle." That was our first conversation.

Nancy says now she tried to give me the brush-off because I had said I was friend of Margie Adler's and she couldn't stand Margie Adler. But I had waited a whole week to meet Nancy, I wanted to be friends with her, I did not notice her attempts at brush-off. Yes she seemed a little aloof, but I didn't know her then, whatever aloof things she did I assumed was part of how she was. It never crossed my mind I was being brushed off. I said "let's have lunch together."

Nancy took me to the Madison Avenue Pub which I loved. I had never eaten in a place like that before, I felt so sophisticated. The cheeseburger was scrumptious. And Nancy told me she lived a block away. She had a small apartment in a brownstone around the corner from Madison Avenue. Over lunch we totally hit it off. And Nancy and I remain best friends to this day.

Sometimes I had lunch with all the other girls who worked there, which was a lot of fun. I liked the place we all had lunch in, I would order a chocolate egg cream or vanilla egg cream with my lunch, and I loved all the girls, they were great. One of them even turned out to be the big sister of a girl who had been in the clique way back at Higley Hill. She was a very pretty girl and very popular girl. Even tho a beautiful Polynesian princess looking girl was the head of the clique, the boys actually chose Phyllis. They were all in love with Phyllis. And Nora turned out to be Phyllis' big sister. Altho Phyllis was tall and Nora was short. Nora was also very pretty.

Nora and I must have gone somewhere together at

night, and we must have been stoned. Because I remember being in a car with her on 14th Street and I said to her "are you stoned?" And she said "why, am I driving badly?" and I thought, 'How do I know how someone is driving,' it never occurred to me to pay attention.

I felt close to Nora because if her sister had been in socialist camp with me it meant her parents were like my parents. Also I felt close to Nora because she told me her boyfriend used to be Melvyn Margolies. Melvyn Margolies was such a complete and total wild man, that even tho Nora seemed so lovely, so pretty, so elegant, so classy, how could she not be a fun natural girl with a boyfriend like that. It was impossible for me to picture them together. I could not see how any girl would go for Melvyn, he was way too wild.

There was another girl who worked there that I liked a lot. She was a blond. She also lived in the area. And during her lunch hour she would go home to walk and feed and pet her huge German shepherd and I went with her. She was devoted to her dog. She was such a nice girl.

She had a problem. The Riverdale Children's Agency was a foster care agency, and many of the children were teenagers. Our job as social workers was to take them out to lunch, ask them how everything is going, and also sometimes to visit the foster home. But mostly to take them out to lunch or take them to nice things. My caseload had some teenaged girls and some children, but her caseload had some teenaged boys. And of course she was beautiful zaftig blond and a very nice person, so the teenaged boys were very attracted to her. They were young men and she was a beautiful blond.

I had a great time when we all went out to lunch together, but as soon as I became best friends with Nancy she and I went to Madison Pub together for cheeseburgers and talked. She liked me very much and invited me to her house around the corner, and soon we had sleepovers. I invited her to my apartment in the East Village and I took her to everything I went to. I took her to an early women's liberation meeting but that didn't work for Nancy. But I took her to The Pageant Players loft to watch them perform, and also to go to their workshops on Wednesday evenings. And she loved The Pageant Players.

We'd go back to my apartment after work. I'd take her to B&H, she loved the food. Then I would put on an outfit and get stoned, Nancy didn't smoke pot. And we'd take the bus to the Pageant Players loft on East Broadway. I remember once getting stoned with Nancy and seeing her with new eyes. "You pretend to be a Jewish social worker" I told her "but really you are Sophia Loren, an Italian actress." Which was astute of me, Nancy was a beautiful actress, and she is the most dramatic girl I ever met, she is thrilling.

Nancy loved the Pageant Players, and once she brought along her friend from Boston College or from Berkeley, Nancy had gone to both colleges. Her friend critiqued The Pageant Players, "the girls are not good but the boys are great." I was surprised at the critique because in my mind the Pageant Players were above criticism, they were a glorious amazing experience. Nancy's friend was like Nancy, and not a little hippie chick like me. She was even more stolid than Nancy. Nancy's stolidness was just a façade, underneath the girl was wild, just as wild as me, but her friend was not.

The first time I took Nancy to Pageant Players she had not known about the 7 flights you have to climb up to get to the loft, and they are long flights. But the next time she remembered.

We stood at the bottom of the steps and she said "I'm not climbing up all those steps." She refused to budge. I did not know what to do. However I was very stoned. I said "Nancy, they moved down to the loft one flight below, it is not such a long climb."

So she said "OK." And when we reached the loft she said, "it's amazing, that one flight makes a big difference."

And I said "they did not move, I made it up."

Getting Nancy to leave for the Pageant Players wasn't that easy either. She had her supper at B&H and for dessert she ordered noodle pudding. When it was time to go to East Broadway, Nancy would say "I cannot move! O that noodle pudding!"

I was high as a kite and said "that's OK Nancy, I'll just ring for the elevator," and marched out the door. Which got her up in a flash, since I lived in a tiny walk-up and there was no elevator.

After we had been friends for a year Nancy said "I have discovered liberation, I stopped wearing my girdle." And I giggled to myself, because of course by this time I had stopped wearing a bra, I couldn't imagine Nancy had been wearing a girdle all this time. Who wears a girdle!

I loved sleeping over at Nancy's house. She would get out negligees for us to sleep in. It was my first negligee, it was so much fun to wear a negligee. And she would make

Rice Crispies with milk and sliced bananas for breakfast which I loved. And one time her old boyfriend from college visited and she cooked us roast lamb. I always had delicious food with Nancy. She took me to the Jewish Institute which was a few blocks from where we worked, and we would have delicious lunches there too. And it was Nancy who introduced me to Ideal Coffee Shop, which was a German restaurant on York Avenue, not far from where she lived. I never had German food before, it was so delicious.

The great thing about Nancy is she was always game, and we had great times together. When women's liberation was invited to a fancy banquet in the art museum in Philadelphia, I went with Jeannie and Ti-Grace, and I took Nancy. We met at Grand Central Station and we were late for the train. I charged down the steps and when I turned around to look for Nancy, I was appalled to see her slowly sailing down on the escalator. When she finally reached bottom she said "O Annie you flew! You should have seen your face when you saw me on the escalator."

Nancy had zero interest in women's liberation but she loved adventure. Jeannie and Ti-Grace talked women's liberation politics the whole train ride, but Nancy's comment was about Ti-Grace. "She wears tiger-striped print dress, very low cut, over left breast she wears button 'Feminism' and her name is Ti-Grace which sounds like tigress. It is extremely provocative and seductive."

A note to all writers, cartoonists, photographers, artists, anyone who wants to publish a book

It is a great gift from heaven that CreateSpace and Lulu.com let any writer publish their book for free, if you do all the work yourself. I was overwhelmed and terrified when I saw all the technical stuff involved, but the angels at the community board at CreateSpace walk all us newbies thru it. And nothing turned out to be as hard as it looked. For those who have extra cash and don't want to do all this work themselves, there are many print-on-demand companies which will do it for you. The beauty of it is now anyone can publish their book. A new universe has opened up for anyone who wants to share .their creativity with the world.

Love, Anne and good luck on your enterprise!

www.ingramcontent.com/pod-product-compliance
Lightning Source LLC
LaVergne TN
LVHW020537100826
845148LV00010B/1499

* 9 7 8 0 9 8 4 0 9 7 6 0 9 *